FOR MY GRANDSON
SHANE MASON

Acknowledgements

Thanks are due to my enthusiastic and indefatigueable editor, Eilís French; to the children from Cloghroe School, Blarney, County Cork, and the children from St Ita's, Corbally, County Limerick, who read and commented on the first draft; and to my friend Cath Thompson, whose comment on the upheaval that Christianity must have brought to fifth-century Ireland inspired me to write this book.

Contents

 # Chapter 1

'Ita, quick! Look! Look at the altar table!'

It was a sunny morning, and Ita and Fergal had just ridden the two miles from Drumshee law school over to the small church at Kylemore. 'Tell Cetterick the priest that the Brehon would like to see him in order to discuss the case of Rory the goldsmith,' Owen, the assistant teacher, had told them. 'Tell him the Brehon will be back from King Carthen's court at about noon.'

'We'll bring Cetterick back with us,' Fergal had said. 'That will give that poor slave boy, Britus, a bit of peace for an hour or so.'

Ita had enjoyed the two-mile ride. Fergal and she were good friends. Fergal had come to Drumshee law school ten years ago, when he was six and she was five, and they had been friends ever since. 'You look like twins – both of you small, dark and clever,' Ita's father used to say when they were little.

When they reached the church, Ita had dawdled, studying the sundial at the gate – it was nearly noon, she saw from the shadow on the stone – but the urgency of Fergal's shout made her turn and dash after him.

It was the first time she had been in the church. Patrick the priest had converted many people to Christianity when he visited Coad eighteen months ago; but Ita's father, Flann, had kept the old religion of Druidism. For a moment, therefore, Ita didn't know where to look for the altar table. Then her eyes adjusted to the grey light coming in through the little window on the eastern side. She took a hesitating step forward and then stopped, a sick feeling in the bottom of her stomach.

The altar was made from white marble, but it wasn't white now. It looked as if someone had taken a paintbrush and smeared blobs and stripes of red paint over it. But it wasn't red paint; it was blood.

And on the altar lay a man – a very small, thin man. His head had been beaten in, but his face was still recognisable.

Ita stared at him. 'Is it Cetterick the priest?' she whispered.

Fergal nodded. He cleared his throat noisily once or twice before the words would come out.

'It's Cetterick all right,' he said.

'Is he . . .?' Ita stopped. The solid lump of porridge

8

that had lain in her stomach since breakfast was starting to rise up. She swallowed hard and kept her eyes fixed on a bit of dark wood on the floor, moving it around and around with her foot, until she felt she could trust her voice.

'Is he dead?' she went on, as steadily as she could.

'He's dead all right,' said Fergal heavily. 'He's been dead for a while, I'd say.' He reached out and carefully touched the hand that dangled over the side of the altar. 'Yes – he's getting cold.'

'Who could have . . .?' Ita didn't finish the question. Many names could have come to their minds. Cetterick, the priest, had been the most hated man in the area around Drumshee. Eighteen months before, when Patrick had baptised Carthen, King of Corcomroe, a large number of people had become Christians. Cetterick had been appointed priest, and the king had taken land from one clan to give to him; there had been a certain amount of bad feeling about that, but if a different man had been priest it might soon have been forgotten. Unfortunately, Cetterick had been arrogant and cruel, and soon everyone had come to hate him. Many of the people who had become Christian had since gone back to the old religion.

Nevertheless, one name sprang immediately to both Ita's and Fergal's lips as they stared at the battered body of the priest.

'Britus!'

'I hope it isn't,' added Ita in a low voice.

'I wouldn't blame him,' said Fergal tensely, 'not after the way Cetterick's treated him. He may be a slave, but ever since Cetterick bought him, he's done nothing but beat that poor boy. He doesn't feed him enough, either.'

'We'd better look for him,' said Ita reluctantly. Her legs trembled, and suddenly she wasn't sure that she wanted to find Britus. Whoever had battered in the priest's head had done so in a frenzy of rage; perhaps Britus was still hiding in a shadowy corner of the little church, with a hammer in his hand, ready to strike again . . .

'We'll have to let your father know,' said Fergal. Ita's father was the Brehon, the judge and lawgiver for the kingdom of Corcomroe. All crimes had to be reported to him.

Ita nodded. The mention of her father steadied her. She and Fergal were both students at the Drumshee law school; they also had to play their part in keeping law and order.

'Let's try the house first,' she said.

Cetterick's small stone cottage was empty of anyone except a cat washing its whiskers in front of the fire.

'Of course,' said Fergal. 'Britus must be with Mahon. He helps him with building his house every Saturday morning.'

'I'd forgotten,' said Ita, relieved. 'Well, if he's with Mahon, he can't have killed Cetterick.'

Up until eighteen months before, Mahon had also been a student at the law school; but then he had been given a rich gift by the king, and he had abandoned the studies that he hated and bought a small farm by Lough Fergus. Until very recently he had still lived at Drumshee, but now that the fine summer weather had come he lived in a small shed on his own farm, and most of his days were spent building his house. He hired Britus from Cetterick once a week to help him.

'We'll go over to Lough Fergus and see. We were going to go there anyway, after we delivered your father's message to the priest,' said Fergal. 'If we don't turn up, Mahon will wonder where we are – and, even if Britus isn't with Mahon, it won't take us too much out of our way. We can just go back to Drumshee along the riverbank and tell the Brehon what's happened.'

But Britus was with Mahon. Small, dark, very thin, very frightened–looking, he was scuttling around with buckets of the lime mortar that Mahon was plastering between the stones of his house.

'Britus,' said Fergal, as they got off their ponies by the lime heap, 'was your master Cetterick all right when you left home this morning?'

The slave boy stared at Fergal. 'Don't be scared,' said Ita gently; she knew Britus spoke the Celtic tongue, but now he looked as if he hardly understood Fergal's words.

'What's wrong?' asked Mahon, coming over to them with the trowel still in his hand.

'Cetterick is dead,' Ita whispered in his ear. 'Murdered.'

'What!' said Mahon. He stared at Britus with horror in his eyes. Suddenly he took a few steps forward, snatched the boy's hand and held it up.

The slave boy's arm was filthy. He looked as if he hadn't washed for a month. Here and there, showing even blacker than the dirt, were the marks of bruises; and on his wrist and upper arm, and on the ragged edge of his tunic, were stains of dried blood.

'I wondered what had happened to him,' said Mahon, to Ita and Fergal. 'I thought he must have had to kill a lamb or something before he came, but he arrived so late, and in such a state, that I didn't bother asking; I just set him to work straightaway.'

'What time did he come?' asked Ita.

'Nearly an hour ago,' said Mahon briefly. He turned to the boy. 'Britus,' he demanded, 'did you kill Cetterick? Did you kill your master?'

Britus shook his head wordlessly. He seemed unable to speak, almost unable to stand. His legs shook under him, and suddenly his teeth began to chatter.

'Put him on my pony, Fergal,' said Ita, looking at the boy compassionately. 'We must get him back to Drumshee; my father will have to see him. I'll walk back with Mahon. You'll come, won't you, Mahon?' she added.

'I'll come,' said Mahon tensely. 'I'm the only one that Britus really knows, now.'

It was true. Britus had been working for Mahon for a couple of months, and Mahon had gradually taught the frightened, abused boy to trust him.

'You ride, Ita,' said Fergal. 'I'll walk.'

'No,' said Ita decisively. She wanted the opportunity to talk to Mahon. He was so busy with his house that she hardly saw him these days. And yet, less than two years ago, they had wanted to be married. It was Flann who had said they would have to wait for a few years; he didn't like early marriages. Since then, it seemed, Ita and Mahon had gradually grown apart. Perhaps it was that her life was so bound up with her studies at the law school, while Mahon had other interests now; but Ita felt that a great gap had opened up between them. She would be glad of an opportunity to be with him, with no one else around. 'You go ahead with Britus, Fergal. He's shivering; tell Fionnuala to give him something hot to drink.'

I hope he's safe on Primrose, she thought, as she watched Fergal and Britus canter away up the hill towards Drumshee. It hadn't occurred to her that Britus might not be able to ride. Cetterick had bought him at the market in Kinvara, but she remembered hearing that he had originally been captured from a settlement near the sea in Britain – Mahon had told her that he was very clever with a boat and caught all the fish his master could eat from Lough Fergus. Perhaps he had never ridden before. *He'll be all right,* she comforted herself; *Primrose is as old as the hills, and very gentle and sure-footed. Fergal will look after him, anyway.* Her eyes followed them until they reached the top of the hill; then she turned back to Mahon.

'He looks so sick,' she said, worried. 'Do you think it was the shock of finding Cetterick? I would have thought that he'd be quite glad to find him dead – unless . . .'

'Unless he was the one who killed him,' finished Mahon. 'The shock of what he'd done might make him look like that. I wouldn't blame him if he did it,' he added. 'I felt like killing Cetterick myself sometimes. Most people have.'

Ita walked beside him in silence. She knew he was right. Cetterick had been a cruel, arrogant man who seemed to enjoy others' unhappiness and pain.

'Britus has blood all over him,' continued Mahon. 'I saw some on the back of his leg, too, when he got on your pony. I'd say he did kill him.'

Suddenly Ita felt a spurt of anger. 'Why are you so sure?' she snapped. 'When you were accused of murder, we all believed in you and went straight to work to prove you were innocent.'

Mahon shrugged his shoulders. He seemed amused by her anger. 'You have to face facts,' he pointed out. 'Just because you're sorry for Britus, that doesn't mean he didn't kill Cetterick. Anyway, don't worry – he won't even be punished for it. He can't pay the fine; he has no goods, no land, no family, nothing. The one who has to pay the fine for a slave's crime is his master – I remember that much from law school – and his master is dead.'

'That's Brehon law,' Ita said unhappily. 'Brehon law says that, if a person does something wrong, he – or his family or clan – has to pay a fine. Will this be judged by Brehon law, though? You know King Carthen is a Christian; what if he decides that, since Cetterick was a Christian priest, Britus will have to pay the penalty that the Christian church has fixed for murder?'

'What!' Mahon stopped so abruptly that he almost lost his balance on the rough ground.

'Well, you know what the Christians say,' Ita said, looking at him intently. 'An eye for an eye; a life for a life. If Britus really killed Cetterick, he'd be condemned to death by their laws.'

'Oh, rubbish,' said Mahon uneasily. He flung a stone at a passing crow, and then started to walk so quickly that Ita had to run to keep up with him. 'Your father would never allow that to happen.'

Ita caught up with him and tucked her hand into his. 'Well, he's having a very difficult time protecting Rory, the goldsmith,' she said. 'You remember what happened? Rory killed that coppersmith from Liscannor in a drunken fight, and Cetterick was trying to persuade my father and the king that Rory

should be hanged. He even offered to do it himself.'
She shuddered as she thought of the scene: her father
standing in the doorway of the schoolhouse,
watching quietly as Cetterick, his voice rising to a
scream, demanded the sacrifice of Rory's life.

'Cetterick's dead now, anyway,' muttered Mahon,
after a few minutes' silence. 'There's no one to look
for Britus's life.' He was still walking very fast, and Ita
let go of his hand. She would walk at her own pace,
she decided stubbornly; let him wait for her or go
ahead, as he pleased. The midday sun was hot on her
head, and she suddenly felt tired and depressed.

'Did I tell you how much silver I got for those
calves I sold in Kinvara?' asked Mahon suddenly,
stopping and turning around to wait for her.

'No,' said Ita sulkily. How could he talk about
calves when poor Britus was in such trouble?

'Two ounces,' said Mahon proudly.

'Oh,' said Ita. She didn't look at him, and she made
no effort to hurry to his side. She was beginning to
wish that she had ridden back with Britus and
allowed Fergal to walk with Mahon. Mahon was so
changed from the boy she had known for six years at
the law school; these days he seemed to think of
nothing but making money and building a splendid
house.

She turned her thoughts away from Mahon and began to worry about Britus. She felt a great sense of pity for him. She herself had so many friends: a father who was devoted to her; Fionnuala, her nurse, who would do anything in the world for her; the boys at the law school, who were all like brothers to her . . . Britus had nothing and no one. He had looked so ill, too. He might become overwhelmed and run away to hide; he might even, in a fit of despair, gallop down to the sea and throw himself in . . . No, she comforted herself: Fergal was very kind and sensitive; he would be careful of Britus. And once they got back to Drumshee, old Fionnuala – who had been Ita's nurse, and her mother ever since Ita's own mother had died – would look after Britus.

'I'm going to buy a pony for myself next week,' said Mahon, who was still waiting for her. 'Then I won't have to ride on the old farm horse.' She could see him looking sidelong at her to see whether she was impressed, but she ignored the look and walked past him.

'Hurry up,' she said curtly. 'I need to see my father; he should be back by now. We have to make sure that Britus is looked after.'

 # Chapter 2

When Ita and Mahon arrived at Drumshee, the enclosure around the law school seemed full of people. The law school itself had been built inside the ancient walls of the Drumshee fort. There were five buildings there: the schoolhouse; the scholars' house, where the boys and Fionnuala and her deaf old husband Donogh lived; the kitchen-house, where they all ate the meals Fionnuala cooked; the assistant teacher's house; and the Brehon's house, where Ita and her father lived. Fergal was standing beside the kitchen-house with Britus; Fionnuala and Donogh were gazing uneasily at the slave boy. Diarmuid – the eldest of the law scholars, a tall, good-looking boy of seventeen – was holding his pony beside the gate of the enclosure. Cathal, Aidan and Ninian were standing in front of the scholars' house holding their hurleys; from time to time Cathal impatiently flicked at a stone with his hurley and then, with a quick glance at his master, Flann the Brehon, checked himself.

Flann stood in front of his house, deep in

conversation with Donal the physician. *Fergal and Britus must have covered the two miles from Lough Fergus very quickly, if Donal's already been called in*, thought Ita. Ita didn't know Donal very well – he had only recently come to the kingdom – but she had heard that he was a clever man. He was speaking in short, decisive sentences, and Flann was nodding his head in agreement.

'Owen,' Flann called. Owen, his young assistant teacher, appeared in the doorway of the schoolhouse. 'Take Donogh and some of the men from the fields, and care for Cetterick's body. We will bury him tomorrow.'

And then there would be the trial and the punishment for his murderer, thought Ita. This slave boy, probably younger than she – he looked barely fourteen – would have to pay the penalty, perhaps the ultimate penalty: a life for a life.

'I'll go back with them,' said Donal the physician. 'I was just about to take my dinner when your young scholar, Diarmuid, arrived. As I live only a few minutes from the church, I went there first, but I thought I'd come back with him after I'd seen the body and knew Cetterick was dead. I just wanted to see you, Brehon, and let you know what I think was the cause and time of death. He must have been killed well before noon – beaten to death, I would say.'

Flann nodded, but said nothing; he was a man of few words. His eyes went to Britus in a long, considering look. Britus flinched and turned back to Fergal.

Flann's eyes moved to his daughter, and he smiled a welcome. Ita left Mahon and ran over to him.

'Don't be too sure that Britus killed him, Father,' she whispered urgently. 'There are plenty of others who would have wanted Cetterick dead.'

Her father looked at her with a glint of amusement. 'I'm never sure of anything, Ita, until I have all the facts before me. Don't forget what I always tell you scholars: the law is there to find the truth.' He didn't wait for a reply, but turned to Diarmuid, who was still waiting in readiness by the gate. 'Diarmuid,' he said quietly, 'go to Drumevin and ask Rory the goldsmith if I may have a word with him.'

So he thinks the same as I do, thought Ita: *it might not have been Britus*. Suddenly she felt a surge of confidence in her father. He would find the truth – and, even if Britus had murdered Cetterick, Flann would try to turn King Carthen's thoughts towards the mercy of Brehon law: a fine, rather than the 'life

21

for a life' of Christian law.

'Ita,' continued Flann, 'tell Fionnuala to give Britus something to eat and drink, and ask Mahon to stay with him. When you've done that, bring the other scholars into the schoolhouse.'

Mahon looked a little disgruntled, Ita thought as she passed on her father's words. It probably seemed strange to him, not to be joining the other scholars in the schoolhouse. But he had made his choice – and he always said that he was much happier as a farmer than he had been when he was learning those endless law texts. Ita made sure that Britus had a seat by the fire in their house, and left Fionnuala bustling about getting soup and hot bread for him; then she returned to the others.

'We're all to go into the schoolhouse,' she said briefly.

'Not fair,' muttered Cathal. 'It's Saturday afternoon! How can we play that match against the McClancy law school if we have no time to practise?'

Ita gave him a sympathetic smile – Cathal's life was hurley; she knew that – and turned to Fergal. 'Has my father questioned Britus?' she asked.

'I told him that Cetterick was dead,' replied Fergal. 'He sent Diarmuid for Donal the physician, and then he asked Britus if he knew who killed

Cetterick. Britus just shook his head, and the Brehon didn't say anything else.'

'That's the trouble with the Brehon,' complained Aidan. 'You never know what he's thinking.'

'A good lawyer keeps his own counsel,' said Ninian pompously. He was the cleverest of them all, and he modelled himself on his master, Flann, whom he admired immensely.

'Where's Bran?' asked Ita.

'In the schoolhouse,' said Cathal contemptuously. 'He couldn't be bothered playing hurley. He's spending his Saturday afternoon getting *extra teaching* from Owen.'

Ita smiled. None of the boys liked Bran; she didn't like him much herself, although he was very good-looking and always dressed in fine clothes and elaborate gold ornaments. He was the same age as Diarmuid − a year older than the other boys − and had been to a law school in Cork before coming to Drumshee; he said that it hadn't been a very good law school, and that his father, who was a Brehon, had taken him away and sent him to Drumshee when Mahon's leaving had opened up a place for a new student. Certainly he was behind the other Drumshee scholars in his studies, but he worked hard to make up the gaps. *I don't trust him, though*, thought

Ita, as she went into the schoolhouse and found a stool across the room from Bran. He was always paying oily compliments to her and to her father, but he was rude and dismissive to the other scholars.

'Sit beside me, Fergal,' she said hastily, as she saw Bran smooth his blond hair and get up to cross the room. Luckily, Ninian took the stool on the other side of her, and Bran sat down again.

'I'm sorry to interrupt your Saturday half-holiday,' said Flann, as he came into the schoolhouse. 'I had planned to interview Rory on Monday about the killing of the coppersmith from Liscannor, but with the news of Cetterick's death, I've decided it would be best to do it today.'

The scholars exchanged glances, but only Fergal found the courage to say, 'So you think there's a connection, Master?'

Flann glanced at him with interest, but did not reply. 'While we are waiting for Rory, we will go through some of the law texts you worked on with Owen while I was away,' he said pleasantly.

Cathal suppressed a groan, and the irrepressible Aidan whispered, 'What fun! On a Saturday afternoon!'

Ita glanced down the line of scholars with affection. Diarmuid smoothing his blond hair; Aidan and Cathal hoping for some amusement; Ninian sharpening his wits; Fergal calmly confident. They had been together for the past seven or eight years, and they were like one family. Sometimes she thought how lonely her life might have been, as a motherless only child, if her father hadn't kept a law school. After the death of Ita's mother, Flann had been so devastated that he had kept his daughter with him, rather than sending her to be fostered as was the custom. As she grew, she had joined in the lessons at the law school, and he had always been very proud of her cleverness. 'There was once a female judge,' he often told her. 'I've read about her judgements. Maybe you'll be one too, and your judgements will be written in the law texts.'

'What have you been studying with Owen this week?' Flann asked.

'The law of persons,' said Ninian rapidly.

'What's the fine for a killing, Bran?' asked Flann.

'Forty-two *sét*s – twenty-one ounces of silver,' said Bran smugly.

'Easy,' whispered Cathal.

'For a secret killing, Cathal?' asked Flann, his eyes fixed on the door.

Cathal coloured and hesitated. He looked an appeal to the others.

'Eighty-four *séts*, or forty-two ounces of silver,' said Aidan, in a very plausible imitation of Cathal's husky voice.

'Answer when you're asked, Aidan,' said Flann, still not taking his eyes from the open door. 'If you want a question so badly,' he added, 'here's one for you: what are the honour-prices for a coppersmith, a silversmith, a blacksmith and a goldsmith?'

There was a silence. Aidan's mouth gaped open. Flann was now looking at the students, so no one dared help him. Under Brehon law, every person had an honour-price, determined by his or her profession and rank; and it was essential to know them all, as penalties and fines for any wrongdoing were fixed according to the victim's honour-price. The problem was that there were so many of them.

'I don't know, Master,' said Aidan eventually. Bran sniggered, and the others looked at Aidan with sympathy: now he was in trouble.

'Good,' said Flann, unexpectedly. He gave the startled Aidan a slight smile. 'I'd always prefer a scholar of mine to admit that he doesn't know something, rather than making a guess. There's no room for guesswork in the law. The honour-price of all four is the same: seven *séts*, or three and a half ounces of silver.'

The questions and answers went on for another half-hour. *Diarmuid's taking a long time finding Rory the goldsmith*, thought Ita. She looked at Fergal with her eyebrows raised, and he whispered, 'Maybe Rory has run away. Maybe he's the one who murdered Cetterick.' Then, smoothly, he said aloud in answer to Flann's question: 'Divorce is permitted to a woman whose husband is cruel to her.'

At that moment they heard the clatter of hooves on the stones outside, and the sound of voices. Diarmuid came into the schoolhouse, followed by the large figure of Rory the goldsmith.

'Sorry to keep you waiting, Brehon,' he said heartily. 'Your young scholar was looking for me at Drumevin, but I was out. He had to wait till I got back.'

Flann bowed politely, and went through a host's ritual of finding Rory a comfortable chair and inquiring whether he wanted anything to eat or drink. It was only when Rory was sitting down, looking quite at ease, that Flann shot the first question at him.

'And where were you?' he asked mildly.

Rory looked taken aback.

'When Diarmuid was looking for you at Drumevin,' explained Flann.

'Oh,' said Rory. There was a moment's silence; it was obvious that Rory was hunting for a likely explanation. 'I was fishing in Lough Fergus,' he said eventually.

Diarmuid's head snapped up and he stared at Rory. *Rory is lying*, thought Ita, *and Diarmuid knows it – how? Will he say anything?*

Diarmuid, however, said nothing, and Flann nodded blandly.

'Could we just go through that unfortunate business in Liscannor?' he said. 'You went there to meet Naoise the coppersmith, and an argument began . . .'

Rory nodded. 'Yes, that was the way of it,' he said eagerly. 'We were talking about things we had made, and boasting a bit, I suppose – we both had drink taken. I suppose we got more and more excited. Anyway, he pulled a knife out of his pocket and waved it around. "Look at that," he said. "Look at the way the light catches it. That's more beautiful than any gold. What good is a gold knife to anyone? Gold is too soft to be any use to real men."'

Rory was speaking easily and fluently, Ita thought; he didn't seem at all uneasy. She glanced at Fergal; he looked sideways at her, raising his eyebrows slightly, and then back at Rory's flushed face. Was that a hint of relief in Rory's face? wondered Ita. Did he know about Cetterick's death? Had he expected to be questioned about that, and been relieved to find that the Brehon was just concerned with the killing of the coppersmith?

'And then?' prompted Flann.

'And then,' continued Rory, 'he jabbed the copper knife in my face, and . . . and I pulled out my iron knife from my pouch, and I said, "Iron is good enough for scum like you," and I stuck the knife into him. I didn't really mean to kill him. I was just in a temper, what with the drink and everything . . .'

'And you stabbed him?' asked Flann.

'I stabbed him,' admitted Rory. 'It was a terrible thing to do – I couldn't believe I had done it . . . I'll never forget it for the rest of my life. I'll happily pay the penalty to his father.'

'The penalty – ah . . . So what is the penalty?' Flann inquired blandly.

Suddenly beads of sweat broke out on Rory's forehead. 'The . . . the . . . the fine,' he said, for the first time stumbling over his words. His eyes avoided Flann's. 'One of your young scholars will be able to tell me. What is it?' he appealed to Diarmuid. 'How many ounces of silver?'

Diarmuid, too well trained to speak without his master's permission, gazed back at him. Rory mopped sweat from his forehead with a large square of fine white linen. He was a rich man, Ita was sure: his tunic was also of the finest linen, dyed an expensive saffron-yellow, and his cloak was lined with marten skins and fastened with a large gold brooch. The money for the fine would be of no importance to him.

'It may not be a question of money,' said Flann, after a long pause. 'Cetterick the priest went to see you, didn't he? And you know what he would have done. He was to see King Carthen on Monday. You know what he would have demanded, don't you? He wanted a life for a life.'

Rory's highly coloured face flushed an even deeper red, then paled. 'No,' he said, with an effort. 'No, I didn't know that was what he wanted.'

He's lying, thought Ita. Cathal's head had whipped around, and he opened his mouth to say something, but she gave him a warning glance and touched her finger to her lips. Cathal was inclined to speak first and think afterwards. Her father would not welcome any interruption at this stage.

'And what do you think would have happened if Cetterick had managed to see the king on Monday?'

inquired Flann quietly.

Rory mopped his face again. 'I don't suppose what he said would have counted with the king,' he said uneasily. 'The king would be more likely to listen to you, my lord.'

'Did you know that Cetterick the priest was found dead at noon today?' asked Flann, as casually as he might have asked if it had been raining earlier.

There was no hesitation in Rory's reply. 'No, my lord,' he said. 'I did not.'

 # Chapter 3

'He's lying,' burst out Cathal, after Rory had left to return to Drumevin.

'When?' inquired Flann.

Cathal looked taken aback. 'When he said that he didn't know Cetterick wanted him hanged,' he said, after a moment. 'I heard Cetterick tell him myself. You know that screaming voice that he has – had, I mean? Well, I was riding down from Knockanedan last night, past Rory's house, and I heard Cetterick; I heard the two of them. He was threatening Rory with hanging – screaming at him – and Rory roared at him, "Get off my property, or I'll kill you with my own bare hands."'

A ripple of excitement went through the scholars. *So it may not have been Britus after all*, thought Ita. *Rory had just as much of a motive, if he knew that Monday was the day Cetterick was going to see King Carthen . . . But I don't want it to be either of them*, she thought. *Rory is a nice man*. He had made a gorgeous brooch for her father's present to her on her tenth birthday, and he had gone to a lot of trouble to design it just as she had wanted it. Perhaps it might be someone else again, she hoped; someone strange to them; someone just passing through the kingdom.

An idea came to her and she turned eagerly to her father, but Fergal spoke first.

'I think,' he said hesitantly, 'that may not have been the only lie Rory told. Did you notice, Master, when you asked him, "And what do you think would have happened if Cetterick had managed to see the king tomorrow?" he didn't seem surprised at you saying "if" and "had managed". You sounded as if it would be impossible for Cetterick to see the king tomorrow, and Rory didn't question that at all.'

'And he answered, "I don't suppose it *would have counted* with the king." He didn't say, "will count,"' burst in Ninian. 'You're right, Fergal: it did sound as if Rory knew Cetterick was dead. Otherwise he would have said something like, "I don't suppose the king *will* listen to him," or "I don't suppose it *will* count with the king."'

'He might just have been following my lead, though,' pointed out Flann. 'Rory is a very polite man; he might not have wanted to correct me.'

'Yes, but,' said Ninian eagerly, 'you said, "You know what he would have done. You know what he would have demanded, don't you?" You even emphasised the word "would" a little each time – I noticed that. I was watching Rory's face, and that didn't seem to puzzle him at all.'

'Yes,' said Flann slowly, 'you're right. I was watching his face as well, and I saw no sign of surprise. Still, it's not evidence – just something to bear in mind.'

'I'd say it was Britus who killed him,' said Bran, with his usual superior air.

'Why?' inquired Flann politely.

'Well,' said Bran, 'a slave is more likely to do something like that than . . . Well, that's what I think, anyway.' His voice trailed away. The others looked at him scornfully. They had all been trained to present solid reasons for their beliefs.

'There's another thing against Rory, as well,' said Diarmuid, his blue eyes thoughtful. 'He didn't tell the truth about what he was doing when I was looking for him at Drumevin. He said he'd been fishing; but when he got back home he had no fish with him, and no rod either.'

'Mightn't have caught any,' said Cathal.

'He wouldn't have left the rod behind,' said Aidan. 'Anyway, the river and lake are teeming with fish these days; even old Donogh could catch a fish now, and he's half blind and as good as deaf and in his second childhood.'

'Let us at least bear this in mind when we are considering the evidence against Rory,' said Ninian, attempting to imitate his master's manner but only managing to sound pompous.

'Well put,' said Flann, suppressing a smile. 'Any other points?'

'I was wondering whether it could have been a stranger passing through,' said Ita hesitantly. 'You see, I was thinking about that beautiful gold plate and gold cup that King Carthen commissioned from Rory to put in the church. Someone might have tried to steal them, and Cetterick might have come in and discovered the person.'

'He kept them in a locked cupboard,' said Flann thoughtfully. 'Fergal, did you notice whether the little cupboard was still locked shut?'

Fergal thought intently for a moment and then shook his dark head. 'No,' he said regretfully. 'I got such a shock when I saw the body that I didn't notice anything else.'

'The ladies are always interested in gold,' said Bran with a light laugh. Ita scowled at him. *He's the one who's interested in gold*, she thought. He was wearing a new torc today, the smooth gold encircling his tanned neck. He caught her looking at it and winked at her, and then arranged his mouth in the special smile that he kept for her. Hastily she turned her eyes to the door, to avoid looking at his smirking face.

'Here comes Owen,' she said with relief.

'Everything all right, Owen?' inquired Flann, as the young man came into the schoolhouse and sat down by his side.

'Yes, everything is arranged for the burial,' said Owen. 'Donal the physician has gone to tell King Carthen the news, and to ask him to send another priest to conduct the burial service.'

'And the weapon – has that been found?' asked Flann.

'He was hit over the head with an iron candlestick. It's a huge thing, bigger than a man; it holds twelve candles. We found it lying under the altar – you know that big marble altar they have at the top of their church?' He hesitated and then went on, 'Did Fergal and Ita tell you that Cetterick's body was lying on the altar? Donal thinks he was put there after he was dead.'

'And the church itself?' asked Ita breathlessly. 'Was anything missing?'

'Yes,' said Owen. 'That was the first thing I noticed – after the body, I mean. That little cupboard behind the altar was broken open, and the gold cup and plate were gone. The funny thing is that Donal says he didn't notice that the first time he went to the church, when Diarmuid fetched him. Did you notice the cupboard, Diarmuid?'

All eyes turned to Diarmuid. He looked puzzled.

'No,' he said, after a pause. 'Maybe I was just looking at the body – it was a bit of a shock to see him lying there on the altar. Anyway, after a minute, Donal told me to go back and tell you that Cetterick was definitely dead, and that he would follow me when he'd finished his examination.'

'Did you see anything or meet anyone on your way back?' asked Flann.

'Just the druid, Master,' said Diarmuid readily. 'I passed his place when I was going along by Kylemore North.'

'Did you say anything to him?' asked Flann sharply.

'No, I didn't,' said Diarmuid, looking uncomfortable. 'You know the way Rua has been a bit peculiar ever since the priest arrived.'

That was true, Ita thought. The arrival of Cetterick had reduced the druid, Rua, from one of the most important and influential men in the kingdom of Corcomroe to a useless old man whom only a few people, like Flann, had still honoured.

Though many people in Corcomroe hated Cetterick, Rua had to be one of the foremost among them.

'Well, he was standing by his well, muttering to himself and waving his arms around,' continued Diarmuid. 'He looked as if he had made some sacrifice, a bird or something; he . . .' Suddenly Diarmuid stopped, and a look of horror came over his face, as if he was just realising the significance of what he had seen. 'He . . . he had blood on his hands.'

Everyone in the room stared at him as he finished simply, 'I just slipped past him and went back to Drumshee as quickly as I could.'

 # Chapter 4

'Take ten minutes in the sun while I go over to the kitchen-house and see whether Britus is fed and rested,' Flann had said, and now the Drumshee law scholars, with Mahon and Owen, sprawled on the warm flagstones in front of the schoolhouse.

'Why not Rua?' argued Diarmuid. 'He looked as crazy as a mad dog when I saw him.'

'Yes, and putting the body on the altar might be meant to show it was a sacrifice,' said Fergal thoughtfully.

'I can't see Britus doing that – putting the body on the altar,' said Ita hopefully. 'If he had committed murder, he'd be so terrified that he would just run away. In fact, I was already thinking it was strange that he came back to you, Mahon, if he did murder Cetterick. You would expect him to run away, maybe go to Liscannor and steal a boat.'

'Perhaps he didn't know where the sea was,' said Bran.

'Oh, of course he'd know,' said Ita scornfully. 'You can smell the sea; you can taste the salt on your lips when the wind blows from the west.'

'Isn't there some sort of terrible punishment in the law texts for a runaway slave?' inquired Mahon.

'What would you know about that?' sneered Bran. 'What do you know about the law?'

'He knows more than you, anyway, birdbrain,' said Cathal, his face flaming to the colour of his red hair.

Ita bit her lips to hide a smile. Mahon had known very little even when he was at law school; though clever, he was cursed with a very poor memory. Still, she wasn't going to allow Bran to sneer at him.

'Mahon spent seven years at Drumshee law school,' she said sternly.

'Whatever you say, darling,' said Bran.

Ita's face turned the same colour as Cathal's. 'Shut up,' she said. 'Who said you could call me "darling"?' *It's a pity that he's not under suspicion, instead of poor Britus*, she thought venomously. *I'm sick of him. Why did he ever come here? We had such good times before he came . . .*

'Don't bother with him, Mahon,' she added quickly, catching Mahon's arm to prevent him from landing a punch on Bran's jaw. 'Let's go back to who killed Cetterick.'

'Rua,' said Diarmuid, firmly sticking to his choice.

'Rory,' said Ninian. 'It's much more logical. Think

of the danger he was in! Cetterick usually got his way with the king. Rory faced being hanged. The fear of death will make a man do anything. And,' he added, holding up a hand and ticking off his points on his outspread fingers, 'that's only point one. Point two is the lie he told about not knowing Cetterick was going to see the king; point three, the lie about not knowing the priest was dead; point four, the probable lie about going fishing.'

'His hair was wet, though,' said Diarmuid suddenly. 'I remember noticing that.'

'There you are, then,' said Ninian triumphantly. 'He got blood on him, either when he killed Cetterick or else when he hoisted the body onto the altar, so he washed it off at the lake. That's what made him think of saying he'd been fishing.'

'What do you think, Mahon?' asked Cathal, still anxious to show Bran that Mahon's opinion was valued at Drumshee law school.

'I'm afraid I still think it was Britus,' said Mahon firmly. 'Sorry, Ita, but you haven't heard Britus talk about Cetterick the way I have. He really hated him, and he was frightened of him. I'd say something snapped and he killed him. Probably Cetterick came into the church, found Britus working there, and began hitting him for no reason, as usual. Britus picked up the candlestick and hit him over the head.

Then he ran away to my place and left the body for someone else to find.'

'What's that?' said Aidan suddenly.

'What?' asked Fergal.

'I thought I saw something move there, just outside the enclosure wall – something red.'

'Might be a fox,' said Cathal. 'Just our luck not to be able to go out today! Malachy from Cahermacon told me that he's going up the mountain with his pack of hunting dogs when the sun goes down.'

'Who do you think it was, Fergal?' asked Ita. She was anxious to distract Aidan and Cathal from the fox. She hated fox-hunting and was always glad when the fox escaped.

'I was wondering about Oisín,' said Fergal tentatively.

'Oisín?' asked Aidan.

'Well, the king did take land from his clan to give to Cetterick to set up his church. All that land in Kylemore, near Lough Fergus, was going to be for Oisín when he married. Now he's going to get married, and there are only ten acres of land to spare for him.'

'Not a great motive for murder,' said Bran contemptuously.

'It does mean the difference between being an

ócaire and being a *bóaire*,' said Fergal quietly. 'That's a big difference to a great many people.'

He was right, Ita knew. In the status-conscious society of Celtic Ireland, the difference between being an *ócaire*, a small farmer, and being a *bóaire*, a large farmer, was a vital one. And she was glad Fergal had pointed it out: it was important that there should be lots of suspects, so all the attention wouldn't be focused on Britus. The thought of his white, sick face made her feel very protective.

'Back inside,' said Owen, rising to his feet. 'Here comes the master with Britus.'

Britus looked no better, Ita thought as they hurried inside after Flann and the boy. *In fact*, she thought, squeezing onto her stool between Fergal and Ninian, *if anything, he looks worse.* She looked appealingly at her father. He was always very fair. Was Britus in a fit state for any harsh questioning? She tried to send the thought across the room to him.

Mahon was standing uncertainly at the door. 'Father,' said Ita urgently, 'shouldn't Mahon stay? He's the only one Britus knows.'

'Do you wish Mahon to stay, Britus?' asked Flann.

The boy nodded, and Mahon sat down beside him and gave him a friendly squeeze on the arm. Ita smiled – this was more like the old Mahon she knew

– and a wave of relief washed over her when he smiled back.

'Your name is Britus,' began Flann, very gently. 'And, Mahon tells me, you are fourteen years old.'

The boy nodded.

'And you were captured in Britain and brought here over a year ago, and sold to Cetterick the priest as a slave?'

Again Britus nodded.

'Are your parents alive?'

He shook his head. 'My father was a Roman soldier,' he said, speaking for the first time. 'He was killed in a battle. My mother was killed by the raiders.'

Poor boy, thought Ita.

'Tell me what happened this morning,' said Flann, his voice still gentle.

Britus said nothing. His brown eyes were full of horror; he twisted his fingers together ceaselessly.

'You got up . . . at what time?'

Britus considered this and then said carefully, 'At daybreak.'

'Look!' whispered Fergal in Ita's ear. He nodded towards the window.

In the winter a piece of oiled linen was fastened over the window, to keep out the cold, but now it was open to the summer air. For a second Ita thought she saw something reddish-gold on the sill; then it vanished. She frowned, puzzled. It couldn't have been a fox − not just outside the window like that. The window was at the height of a man's shoulder; unless a fox had jumped onto the sill, she wouldn't have been able to see it. *Maybe it was a stoat*, she thought.

'And then?' Flann persisted. 'What did you do then?'

A long pause; then Britus muttered, 'Lit the fire.'

'So you lit the fire,' encouraged Flann. 'You got the breakfast. And then?'

No answer. The boy bit his lip and shook his head. *He's trying to stop himself crying*, thought Ita.

'Well, let's skip that.' Flann's tone had hardened slightly. He was running out of patience; his scholars, recognising the signs, shifted uneasily on their seats. 'You went to Mahon, by arrangement with your master Cetterick, to help him build his house. You arrived there . . . when?'

Again Britus didn't answer. With an impatient sigh, Flann turned to Mahon. 'What time did he arrive, Mahon?'

'About an hour before noon,' said Mahon readily. 'I know because I was expecting Ita and Fergal about noon, and I expected Britus earlier; I'd planned that the two of us would mix the lime mortar and have it ready when the others arrived to help. I kept going out and looking to see if he was coming, so I know when he arrived.'

'Did he say anything?'

Mahon shook his head.

'How did he look?'

Mahon hesitated.

'It's best to tell the truth always,' observed Flann. 'Lies lead to complications.'

'He seemed in a bit of a state,' said Mahon shortly. 'But then, he often does,' he added. His face darkened and he clenched his fist; Ita knew he was thinking of all the terrible beatings that Britus had suffered.

'Now, Britus,' said Flann sternly, turning to the slave boy, 'you are going to have to answer the rest of the questions yourself. Tell me exactly what happened this morning. Was Cetterick the priest alive when you left him to go to Mahon, or was he dead?'

Britus stared at him. There was stark terror in his eyes. He looked like an animal in a trap.

'You quarrelled with your master? Perhaps he hit you, threatened you — was that it?'

No answer. The boy's chest heaved in and out as if

46

he had been running. The room was so silent that the sound of his breathing seemed to fill it.

'And then you picked up the candlestick and hit him over the head?' went on Flann, his voice still matter-of-fact.

The silence went on and on.

The sound, when it came, made them all jump. It was something between a groan and a scream – like a sound that a spirit from the Otherworld might make, Ita thought – and it burst forth from the slave boy. Then Britus jumped to his feet and hurled himself at the open door.

'Stop him!' shouted Owen, and Mahon flung himself after the boy.

He was not needed, however. A girl suddenly appeared in the doorway, the sunlight illuminating her extraordinary hair. She spread out her arms; Britus, his way blocked, stopped abruptly. She took him by the hand.

'Sit down again, Britus,' she said gently. 'I am here to help you.'

 # Chapter 5

She was the most beautiful girl Ita had ever seen. She was about Ita's age, fifteen, but far taller than Ita, and as slender and graceful as a young willow. Her hair was like spun gold, with threads of red deepening and intensifying its brightness; it stood out from her face in a dazzling cloud. The face was a perfect oval, milk-white, with eyes like pools of brilliant green — the green of young beech leaves in the spring — fringed with black, gold-tipped lashes. She glanced briefly at Ita, then at the stunned boys, and last of all at Flann; then she smiled, a sweet smile that showed lips the colour of rosebuds and teeth as white as sunlight reflecting off polished silver.

'May I come in?' she asked, and her voice was as soft and musical as a low note from a flute.

'Bring the lady in, Mahon,' said Flann. He didn't sound surprised — he never did — but all the others' mouths were open in shock.

'S-sit here,' stuttered Owen, still dazed, but hastily carrying forward his chair.

The girl sat down and turned to Flann. 'My name is Mara,' she said, and then waited.

Flann waited too, but this girl seemed well able to

play him at his own game. She glanced around the room with great self-possession, giving each of the boys a long look and finally coming back to Mahon. She looked deep into his eyes and gave him another of her glorious smiles. He looked dazzled, enchanted, Ita thought resentfully. She had never seen him look at her like that.

'And you are a friend of Britus,' went on Flann.

Mara turned back to him. 'I am the daughter of Cetterick,' she said simply.

Another shock ran through the room. No one had known that Cetterick had been married. Ita glanced at her father, and for a moment she caught a look of astonishment in his eyes; then he was himself again, giving away nothing.

It was Aidan who blurted out, 'I didn't know Cetterick was married!' Flann gave him a reproving glance, but Aidan was too occupied in staring at the beautiful Mara to notice.

'Oh, yes,' said Mara. 'He was married. When he decided to become a priest, almost two years ago, the bishop told him to put away my mother as if she were an evil spirit – "sinful" was the way he put it. I suppose he thought I was sinful, too. From the day he became a priest, my father never came to see either of us.'

For a moment the honeyed sweetness of the strange girl's voice turned harsh, and the bright-green eyes sparked with anger. Then Mara smiled again. All of the boys leant forward. They seemed mesmerised by her beauty.

'Ah,' said Flann, his voice quiet and neutral as always. 'And where have you and your mother been living?'

She hesitated for a moment. 'Near Inchicronan Lake, with my mother's father,' she said eventually.

'Quite a long way to come – seven miles at least,' commented Flann. 'Why did you come?'

She faced him boldly. 'To demand some silver from my father,' she said. 'My mother and I are very poor. My grandfather has little to spare for us.'

Flann nodded. He seemed to lose interest in Mara; he turned back to Britus, with a long, considering look.

'Britus, I'll ask you again: did you hit Cetterick over the head with a candlestick? Did you kill him?'

Mara showed no shock at the words, not a tinge of surprise. *She knew her father was dead*, thought Ita. *Did she just overhear us talking? Or did she know already?*

Mara placed her hand on the slave boy's wrist, gave him a cautionary glance and spoke directly to Flann. 'No, my lord,' she said. 'Britus did not kill my father.'

Flann waited for a moment. His eyes had left Britus and rested on Mara.

'How do you know?' he asked, his voice still calm and neutral.

'Because I saw and spoke to my father after Britus had left,' said Mara confidently.

Flann gazed at her, his hazel eyes as intent as those of a cat watching a mouse. 'Did you kill him, then, Mara?' he asked eventually.

Bran stopped admiring the brooch on his tunic, Mahon started from his stool, Diarmuid stared indignantly; Cathal muttered something and turned red, Aidan's mouth dropped open, Ninian raised his eyebrows; only Fergal and Ita made no move.

Mara, however, showed no shock, no fear. There was even a hint of triumph and amusement in those brilliant green eyes.

'Britus didn't kill Cetterick, my lord,' she repeated, ignoring his last question. 'My father was still alive when Britus left to go to Mahon. I was with my father then, and I saw Britus leave.'

Flann sat back in his chair and studied the flower-like face before him. 'I think,' he said quietly, 'you had better tell me the whole story.'

'Yes, my lord,' said Mara. She lowered her

eyelashes for a moment, as if to hide the glint in her sparkling green eyes.

'I decided to come to see my father,' she began. 'I could no longer bear to see my mother suffer want while he lived in the midst of plenty. When I arrived, he was in the church watching his slave boy, Britus, scrub the floor. I told him I wanted to speak to him, and asked him to come outside the church so that we could be alone together.'

She's learnt this off by heart, thought Ita, noticing the fluent way the story poured from the girl. *She's like one of the bards at the fair at Coad. Even the pauses are calculated for effect.* She glanced at Fergal and was comforted to see one eyebrow raised sceptically. At least one of the boys wasn't totally under Mara's spell.

'He did come outside with me,' continued Mara, 'but he was very angry. He said that I shouldn't have come, that I shamed him by my presence; that I should tell no one that I was his daughter. I asked for even one piece of silver, but he refused. He shouted at me and tried to strike me.' She paused and said, slowly and dramatically, 'I was so angry that I could have killed him – but I was also frightened of him. I ran away and hid behind the gorse bushes.'

'And then?'

'And then he went back to the church door and shouted to Britus, "Go to Mahon and earn some money!" – that must be you,' she added, giving Mahon a dazzling smile. Mahon reddened, and Mara turned back to Flann with an air of secret enjoyment.

'I watched Britus cross the hill and go down towards the half-built house beside the lake. I waited until my father had gone back into the church, and then I set out towards home. I had gone about a mile when my courage began to come back. I thought of how disappointed my mother would be if I came back with nothing, and I decided to try again.'

'So you came back,' prompted Flann.

'Yes, my lord,' agreed Mara demurely.

'And when was that?'

'About a quarter of an hour before noon, my lord.'

'And you spoke to Cetterick?'

'No, my lord, I could not speak to him. He was dead.'

Mara's green eyes flashed around the room. She seemed satisfied with the sensation she had created, so she finished rapidly: 'I saw two people' – a warm smile for Fergal, and a cool glance at Ita – 'go into the church and then cross over towards the house near the lake. I was going to return home – I wanted nothing to do with any investigations into my father's death; I was glad he was dead, glad that someone had killed him! – but then I thought I'd better make sure that Britus wouldn't be blamed, so I followed them here and listened outside to find out what was happening. I made up my mind that I would steal away again if Britus wasn't in any danger.'

So she was the 'fox' Aidan had seen. There was, in fact, something fox-like about this girl, Ita thought. It had been the top of her head that Fergal and Ita had seen through the window; Mara had deliberately waited until Britus had reached the end of his tether before making her dramatic appearance.

'And so you came to tell us what you knew of your father's death,' said Flann. He paused for a moment and then asked casually, 'Perhaps, after Britus had left to go to work with Mahon, you returned to the church and you and your father quarrelled; and in your anger – your justifiable anger – you picked up the candlestick and hit Cetterick over the head? Perhaps you didn't mean to kill him; perhaps you were even defending yourself.'

Mara faced him without a tremor of anxiety. 'How could I do a thing like that to my own father, my lord?' she asked softly.

'That's not an answer,' Fergal whispered, almost soundlessly, in Ita's ear. She nodded, her eyes on her father. Surely he wasn't going to accept that as an answer?

However, it seemed that he was. He had got to his feet. 'We can't let you walk all the way back to Inchicronan,' he said politely. 'Owen, will you go with Mara? Take Ita's pony; you can lead it back.'

'Thank you, my lord,' said Mara softly; then she added, very sweetly, 'I would like to take Britus back with me. Now that my father is dead, he must belong to my mother.'

'Not if her mother's been divorced,' whispered Ninian. He was as dazzled by Mara as the others, but the law was always important to him.

Flann considered the matter and then nodded. 'I'll need to see you both again, but I'll send for you when I need you,' he said. 'Would you be able to manage two ponies on your way back, Owen, if we lend one to Britus as well?'

'I'll go with them,' offered Mahon eagerly. 'I'd like to − I'm not busy at the moment. I'll bring the second pony back.'

'I thought he was busy with his house,' muttered Ita, getting to her feet and tucking her stool under the table. Fergal gave her an understanding look, and she flushed a dark red as she saw the sympathy in his eyes. Mahon had already followed Mara out of the schoolhouse.

Everyone went out to see Mara and Britus depart. Ita made sure that Britus, not Mara, took Primrose, and averted her eyes from the sight of Mahon carefully helping Mara onto one of the other ponies. The last she saw of them was Owen riding down the avenue beside Britus, and Mahon's dark, rough head very close to the flaming gold of Mara's.

She turned to her father abruptly. 'Are we going to discuss Mara's statement?' she demanded, hearing a harsh, aggressive note in her voice.

Flann ignored her. 'Bran, would you ride down to Donal's house and see if he's back? If he is, ask him if he could meet me at Kylemore, at the church, at sundown. I would like to see the place for myself.'

'Will we come with you, Master?' asked Ninian.

'Yes,' said Flann, after a minute's consideration.

'And then we'll discuss Mara's evidence,' persisted Ita.

'And then we'll discuss all the evidence so far,' said Flann gravely. His eyes held amusement, and Ita flushed.

'I'm going to see Fionnuala,' she said, and went quickly into the kitchen-house before any more could be said.

'Where's Mahon going?' asked Fionnuala, as she came in. Fionnuala had looked after Ita almost all her life, and she knew every thought in Ita's head.

Ita shrugged. 'Did you see that girl?'

'To think of her being Cetterick's daughter!' said Fionnuala in a whisper, pulling two stools up to the fire and preparing for a long gossip. 'Did you ever hear of such a thing?'

In spite of her gloom, Ita had to smile. Fionnuala never let anything pass her by. She must have spotted Mara and then listened at the door.

'She's very pretty, isn't she?' she asked, with as much indifference as she could manage.

Fionnuala sniffed. 'Cheap-looking, I thought. I didn't like all that hair floating around. She should plait it. She'd look better that way, in my opinion.'

Ita examined her own black plaits. She was beginning to feel better, but she didn't think any of the boys would agree with Fionnuala.

'Mahon seemed to think she was something special,' she said, and she couldn't keep the slight quiver out of her voice.

Fionnuala sniffed again. 'That's just novelty,' she stated firmly. 'Men are always like that – interested in anything new. He'll be tired of her soon. There's only one girl Mahon cares about.'

'Let me help you with the supper,' said Ita, finding that she did not want to talk to Fionnuala about Mahon after all. 'My father wants us all to go over to Kylemore at sundown, and we'd better have our supper first or all the boys will be getting hungry.'

'Will you eat with the boys or with the Brehon?' asked Fionnuala, busily chopping sorrel to add to the pot of deer meat.

'I'll eat with my father,' said Ita, taking wooden plates and cups from the cupboard on the wall. The boys would probably all be discussing Mara, and she didn't think she could bear that.

When the meal was ready, she carried two covered plates over to the Brehon's house. The deer meat was good, but she had little appetite. Her mind was filled with the picture of Mahon, side by side with the beautiful Mara, riding off to Inchicronan Lake.

'Try to eat a little more,' said Flann. 'Fionnuala will be upset if you leave all that on your plate.'

'I'm not hungry,' said Ita. She hoped he wouldn't say anything about Mahon. She could feel tears pricking at the backs of her eyes.

'Would you like a game of chess?' he asked. 'You beat me last time; you'll have to let me get my revenge.'

'All right,' said Ita, making an effort to rouse herself. Usually she loved chess; she was the best of all the scholars at it. 'Let's use the king's set.'

The king's chess set was very special. It had been presented to Flann by King Carthen, eighteen months before, and it had been specially made by the king's own craftsmen. The light-coloured pieces were made of polished silver, the dark ones of copper. Each set of pawns was made in the likenesses of the eight students who had been at the law school then: Owen, Diarmuid, Aidan, Cathal, Fergal, Mahon, Ninian – there were even a silver and a copper one with plaits, which were meant to be Ita. As she took the tiny pawns out of the box, she couldn't help smiling, and suddenly she began to feel better.

One by one she took out the other pieces and set them on the board's alternating squares of silver and copper. Then she stopped and frowned. There were sixteen copper pieces, but only fifteen silver ones.

'There's a silver rook missing,' she said, consternation in her voice.

'There can't be,' said Flann. 'I always put them away so carefully. When was the last time I used it?'

'It was the night of the midsummer festival,' said Ita. 'Don't you remember? You were playing with Rua, the druid.'

'That's right,' said Flann. 'I beat him, and he wasn't too pleased – he's always a bad loser. As soon as I said, "Checkmate," he got up and said he had to go. I went out to the gate with him and . . . Yes, I remember now: when I came back, the pieces had been put away in the box. I thought you had done it.'

Ita shook her head. 'No,' she said. 'I don't think I would have done that; I would have left them until you came back, and asked you about the game. Anyway, I wasn't in the house when you finished playing. I'd gone up to the goddess Brigid's shrine with . . . with Mahon. I remember because we saw Rua going down the lane.'

Flann frowned. 'That piece is very valuable,' he said unhappily. 'Who could have taken it? Who was here that night?'

'Everyone,' said Ita. 'Because of the festival. All the scholars, Donal the physician, Rory the goldsmith, Cathal's friend Malachy, Oisín – all the neighbours – Fionnuala, Donogh . . . It could have been anyone.'

'Let's leave it for the moment,' said Flann, rising to his feet. 'Put the pieces back in the box. Those boys have finished eating; I know by the amount of noise they're making. If we set off now, we'll have time to see Rua on the way to the church. I'll have to think about this later. It's not a good feeling, to think that we have a thief as well as a murderer among us.'

 # Chapter 6

The great Kylemore forest started near the shores of Lough Fergus. At the edge of the forest was the sacred grove where Rua the druid lived. Unlike the Christians, the druids and their followers saw no need for churches – they worshipped the gods of the sun and the moon, and the springs and the trees, amongst the oak groves of the forest.

Unexpectedly, Ita felt better on the ride to Kylemore. Aidan and Cathal were in wild spirits. As Flann rode ahead, a sombre, thoughtful figure, they began to tease Diarmuid about Mara – first quietly and then, as the distance between them and their master lengthened, more exuberantly.

'Didn't even look at him, did she, Cathal?' said Aidan.

'Didn't notice the way he had combed his hair so carefully,' chimed in Cathal, with an eye on the flush spreading up Diarmuid's tanned neck.

'Mara's even better-looking than Nessa, isn't she, Diarmuid?' asked Aidan.

She is, thought Ita. Until she saw Mara, she had

thought that Nessa — now married to Finbar the horn player and living at King Carthen's court — was the most beautiful girl she had ever seen.

'His face used to go even redder for Nessa, though, didn't it?' inquired Cathal in an interested tone.

'Such a shame the girls never like him,' said Aidan sympathetically. 'Nessa never even noticed him, and now Mara doesn't think much of him either.'

'Shut up!' shouted Diarmuid, and aimed a swipe at Aidan.

'She just kept smiling at Mahon,' said Ninian. Fergal glanced sideways at Ita, but she forced herself to laugh.

'Never mind, Diarmuid,' she said with mock sympathy. 'The next time she comes, you can wear your new tunic and your gold brooch.'

'No good,' said Fergal. 'If she likes gold, Bran's the one she'll go for.'

'Speaking of Bran,' said Ita, 'isn't it great to be without him?' Bran hadn't come back from his errand to Donal; obviously he had stayed to eat at Donal's house and would meet them at the church.

'I wonder if he'll move on to another law school,' said Diarmuid, seizing the opportunity to turn the conversation away from Mara. 'He must know none of us like him; he has no friends.'

'Sometimes I almost feel sorry for him,' said Fergal seriously.

'We're too far above him in knowledge and intelligence,' said Ninian loftily. 'It would be impossible for him to be a friend of ours.'

Ita laughed. Suddenly her mood lifted. To her, the most important things in the world were the law school and the companionship of the other scholars; and she still had those.

'Slow down,' she said. 'My father's turned off the road. We're going to see Rua the druid.'

Rua lived in a small grove of oak trees. It was a silent, mysterious place at the end of summer; no birds sang there, and the trees grew so thickly that almost no light fell on the mossy path that led to the centre. In the heart of the grove was a circle of thirteen standing stones of white limestone, with a flat white table-stone in the middle. Ita never saw this circle without a shiver of fear. The spirits of the Otherworld seemed very near in this sacred place.

Beyond the circle, in the shadowy depths of the oak grove, was a small wooden hut. Outside its door stood Rua, watching their approach. He was a tall, thin man with a deeply lined face; according to the practice of the druids, the front half of his head was shaved from ear to ear. In his hand he held a small iron knife.

'Greetings, Druid,' said Flann, dismounting from his horse and bowing low. All of his scholars followed his example.

'Welcome, Brehon,' said the druid. 'Will you come into my home?'

'Wait here,' commanded Flann, throwing the bridle of his horse to Diarmuid.

'Why can't we go in and listen?' whispered Cathal.

My father has too much respect for the druid to allow his scholars to be present, thought Ita. She put her finger to her lips and then touched her ear. It made no difference whether they were inside or outside; the hut was so flimsy that they could hear every word of the preliminary greetings.

'You have heard of the death of Cetterick, the priest?' asked Flann, after a minute's silence.

'I have heard,' agreed Rua.

'Who told you?' asked Flann. His voice was quicker, sharper.

'I know many things,' said Rua. Ninian pulled a twig from an overhanging branch with an impatient sigh; Diarmuid gave him a warning glance.

'You saw the body,' stated Flann. Fergal gave an excited half-smile. He always loved cross-questioning.

There was a moment's pause; then Rua's deep, gravelly voice agreed, 'I saw the body.'

'By chance?' asked Flann.

Rua did not reply.

'By chance?' asked Flann again.

'Nothing happens by chance, Brehon,' said Rua gravely.

'It is true,' agreed Flann, and waited.

This ready agreement seemed to have softened Rua; he was the next to break the silence.

'I went for a walk,' he volunteered. 'I saw Donal, the physician, at the door of that building they call a church. When he had gone, I went in. The sacrifice was laid on the altar-table. But was it a sacrifice to his god, or to one of ours? Tell me that, Brehon.'

'You saw Cetterick?' queried Flann.

'I saw him.'

'And he was dead.'

'He was dead,' said Rua gravely.

'So you can help me no further?' asked Flann, and from the sound of his voice his scholars knew that he had risen to his feet. They all drew back a little from the hut and were busy studying the branches of the oak trees when the two men appeared.

'Wait,' said Rua, as Flann took his bridle from

Diarmuid. He went back into the hut and returned almost instantly.

'If it is help that you need, Brehon,' he said, 'I can help you.'

From his pouch he took a bundle of sticks. Ita bit her lip. These were the sacred wands of yew. They had words in Ogham, the ancient Celtic language, carved upon them; the straight lines forming the letters stood out black against the wood. When the druid threw them on the table-stone, they would form an answer to any question he asked. Ita felt herself trembling, and the faces of the boys around her looked scared and white. Rua very seldom used these wands of yew; and yet something in the back of her mind told her that she had seen one of them recently.

'You want to know who killed that abomination of the gods?' cried Rua, so suddenly that everyone, except Flann, started nervously. He raised the yew wands high in the air and then flung them on the table-stone. The thin shapes lay like dark stains on the white of the limestone.

Rua approached the table and bent over it, without touching the sticks. His lips moved, but no words could be heard. After a long minute he straightened and turned to face Flann.

'That is a question, Brehon,' he said, 'that is better

not answered.' Without another word, he turned and went back into his hut.

Flann mounted his horse and led the way back through the oak grove in silence. The others followed, awe keeping them silent as well. They had almost reached the end of the grove when a great shout halted them.

'Brehon!' called Rua. 'Talk to your new boy – the fair-haired one. Ask him why he was at the church this morning. Why did he come? What did he do?'

Flann held his horse still for a moment, but Rua had nothing more to say. He went back towards his hut, and Flann rode on to the edge of the grove and turned down the road towards the little church.

'Bran – did he mean Bran?' asked Aidan in a low voice, with a wary eye on Flann's back. 'Maybe that was what he saw in the sacred wands. Maybe he thinks the master won't want the question answered if the answer is one of his own students. Maybe it was Bran who . . . who killed Cetterick.'

'Never,' said Diarmuid. He didn't like Bran much, but he was soft-hearted.

'It wouldn't matter if it was Bran, though, would it?' said Fergal. 'After all, his father must be quite rich, judging by Bran's clothes and his jewellery. He could pay the fine; Bran would go back to Cork, and we'd all be happy again.'

'Yes, but,' said Ita, 'will the crime be judged by Brehon law, or by Christian law?'

Ninian looked interested. 'Master,' he said politely, catching up to Flann, 'we were wondering if the murder of Cetterick the Christian priest would be judged by Brehon law or by Christian law.'

Flann looked at him blankly. 'That is another question to which we don't know the answer.'

They had reached the church. 'He's getting as mysterious as Rua,' whispered Aidan, jumping down from his pony and grinning at Ita.

Ita didn't smile back. Suddenly she was struck by a look of age on her father's face. He did not like this changing of the ancient ways. Alive, Cetterick had brought great trouble to the kingdom; it looked as if his death was going to bring even more.

 # Chapter 7

The church at Kylemore was a small lime-washed building, not much bigger than the schoolhouse at Drumshee. Donal was already there, and Bran was with him.

Ita gave Bran a long look. Was he capable of murder? With any of the other boys she would instantly have said no – but Bran she didn't know him well enough to be sure. She didn't think he would be, though. He seemed more interested in clothes and jewellery than anything else. And why would he have wanted to kill Cetterick? He hadn't hated the priest in the way that Finn, or Rua, or Britus, or even Cetterick's daughter Mara had hated him.

Bran felt Ita's eyes on him, smiled his special oily smile and then winked. She flushed and turned away. *I hope he gets into some sort of trouble anyway*, she thought venomously.

'And the body was found here?' asked Flann, indicating the altar.

'Just here,' replied Donal, 'but I don't think that's

where he was killed. There's not enough blood on the altar – just some smears; if he had been killed there, the blood would be all over it, dripping down onto the floor. He was probably killed over there, by the window, and then carried to the altar. Look: the flagstones under the window are still slightly damp. Someone washed that floor today – probably washed blood off it.'

'Yes, Ita?' said Flann, as she stepped forward and waited his permission to speak.

'I just remembered what – what Mara was saying,' Ita said. 'She told us that Britus was washing the floor, and Cetterick told him to go off and earn some money by helping Mahon.'

'Well remembered – you students are a great help to me,' said Flann, just concealing a proud smile. He looked a bit more cheerful, though from time to time his eye rested on Bran in a long, thoughtful look. 'And the weapon, this candlestick – let's look at that.'

Silently Diarmuid picked up the candlestick and held it out. It was a huge, solid piece of iron, made to hold a dozen candles; it was so heavy that it wobbled dangerously for a moment in Diarmuid's grasp. Flann eyed it with interest.

'Ita, see if you can hold it,' he said unexpectedly. The boys all looked surprised.

He's thinking about Mara, thought Ita instantly. *He must doubt her evidence — must want to test whether she could have struck the blow that killed her father.* She stepped forward readily. 'I'll try, Father,' she said.

'Wait a moment,' said Flann. 'Diarmuid, you carry it outside — come on, all of you. Take it right over next to that gorse bush, Diarmuid. Now, Ita, take it from him.'

Carefully Diarmuid handed the candlestick to Ita, supporting it with one hand while she grasped it firmly with both of hers.

'You can let go, Diarmuid; I can hold it,' she said resolutely. The weight was almost crushing, but she tried her best not to let the strain show in her face.

'Now see whether you can bring it down on that gorse bush,' said Flann. 'That bush is about the height of Cetterick; he was a small man. Don't worry if it falls; just hit that gorse bush with all the force you can manage.'

Ita drew in a long breath, tensed all the muscles in her shoulders and arms, swung the candlestick and brought it down on the gorse bush in front of her. The falling weight wrenched the candlestick from her hands, but the experiment had worked: the gorse bush was almost flattened by the blow.

'So a woman could have killed Cetterick,' said Ita steadily, her eyes on her father's face.

'Or a boy,' said Bran quickly.

'Or an old man,' added Diarmuid. He was still thinking about Rua the druid, Ita thought.

'Or, most likely of all, a strong, fit young man in a state of fear or anger,' observed Donal thoughtfully. 'Still, I mustn't try to take over your profession, Brehon. I'll stick to my own – you'll forgive me for saying that I consider it to be more important.'

'I would say myself that both are important,' said Flann mildly. 'Without the rule of law, mankind would be as the beasts of the forest, swayed by greed and self-interest. If man is to live in a society, laws are necessary. I think we'll have to agree that both our professions are of importance to mankind, Donal.'

'The law must be upheld at all times, in all circumstances and in all places,' quoted Ninian, his narrow, clever face shining with enthusiasm. Sometimes Ita thought that he memorised every word Flann uttered.

'And the law is there to find the truth,' chimed in Fergal.

'I'll leave you to sort out the truth about this

death, then,' said Donal with his frosty smile. 'I must go and attend to the living.'

Flann watched him thoughtfully as he disappeared down the road, the strong-boned horse bearing his master's large frame with ease. Then he turned to his students.

'Well,' he said, 'who killed Cetterick? I'd be interested in your opinions — supported by reasons, of course.'

'Britus,' said Bran. As Flann raised an eyebrow, he said hurriedly, 'He's a slave; he wanted his liberty. It makes sense.'

'What about Mara's evidence?' asked Ita scornfully.

Bran shrugged. 'What's to have stopped Britus going back after she had left and murdering Cetterick then?' he said. He wasn't being quite as oily towards her since he had seen the beautiful Mara, Ita noticed. A day earlier, he wouldn't have disagreed with her like that.

'Possible,' admitted Flann.

'I think it might be Rory,' said Ninian. 'A lot of evidence seems to point in his direction.'

'But Rory's such a nice man,' Ita said, and then wished she hadn't; it didn't sound very intelligent.

'He might be,' said Ninian judiciously, 'but fear will make people do things they wouldn't do otherwise. And Rory was in fear of losing his life: Cetterick might have persuaded the king to have him hanged for the death of the coppersmith.'

'Any other ideas?' asked Flann. Cathal and Aidan shook their heads; Fergal opened his mouth and then, with a quick look at Ita, shut it again; Ita avoided her father's eyes and looked at the ground.

'I wonder whether we should consider the druid, Master?' asked Diarmuid, with a cautious glance at Flann. 'He might not have considered it wrong to kill Cetterick. You heard what he said about a sacrifice. He might have considered this killing to be a sacrifice to the sun god.'

'What do you think, Ita?' asked Flann.

'I don't want to guess,' said Ita impatiently. 'I think we need to gather all the evidence and then sit down and evaluate it. Maybe someone else saw Cetterick alive after Mara left him. All we know now is that he was dead at noon.'

'Well said,' praised Flann; then he went on, swiftly and without changing his tone, 'You'll be able to help us there, Bran. I understand you were here this morning – sometime before noon, I think.'

Bran gulped. Ita, watching him closely, saw a look of definite alarm flit across his face. A minute later she wondered whether she had imagined it; Bran gave a light laugh and said, 'I've been here quite often, Master. As you know, my father has become a Christian, and now he wants me to do the same.'

Flann nodded. He didn't seem surprised, Ita thought, though this was the first she had heard of Bran wanting to become a Christian. She glanced at the other boys; they all looked taken aback.

'So you saw Cetterick that morning,' went on Flann. 'Was he in good health, good spirits?'

Bran hesitated. 'No, Master,' he said eventually. 'I didn't see him. When I got near the church, I heard voices – people outside the church – so I went away.'

'Voices?' asked Flann. 'Whose voices? You would know Cetterick's voice.'

'I think it may have been Cetterick and his daughter,' said Bran, after a moment's thought. 'It was hard to hear; they were just murmurs.'

'And you saw Britus,' stated Flann.

Again the hesitation; but eventually Bran nodded. 'I saw him later,' he said briefly.

'When?' Cathal demanded aggressively. *He really hates Bran*, Ita thought.

Bran shrugged. After a moment he answered, 'A little way down the road I looked back – I was wondering who had been with Cetterick – and I saw Britus.'

'May I ask a question, Master?' asked Fergal politely.

'Yes, indeed,' replied Flann, with equal courtesy.

'Bran, when you did see Britus, where was he? Was he going towards Lough Fergus, towards Mahon's house?'

Bran faced him with a hint of triumph in his eyes. 'No,' he said. 'He was standing by the corner of the church. I didn't see him move.'

'Show us,' commanded Flann.

Bran led the way reluctantly. 'Here,' he said, passing the door to the church and going around to the side of the building.

'Where were you?' asked Ninian.

Bran glanced back over his shoulder to the gorse bushes where they had been standing; then, unexpectedly, he pointed in the opposite direction. 'Over there,' he said.

'May I test this, Master?' asked Aidan. Without waiting for an answer, he went on rapidly: 'Ita, you're about the same size as Britus. You stand here, and I'll go over to where Bran was.'

In a second, Aidan's long legs had covered the distance. He called back, 'I can't see Ita – not even the top of her head. The other corner of the building is blocking me.'

'I must have been a bit further over,' said Bran impatiently. 'All I know is that I heard voices – yes, I'm sure they were Cetterick's and Mara's – and I saw Britus hiding.'

'Why didn't you mention this earlier?' asked Flann mildly.

'I didn't want to get Britus into trouble, Master,' replied Bran sweetly. 'Ita seemed concerned about him,' he added.

'Don't make that rude sound, Cathal,' said Flann sharply. 'If you disagree with Bran, then say so politely.'

'Well,' said Cathal, his face as red as his hair, 'Bran has done nothing but try to get Britus into trouble. He said over and over that he thinks Britus did it – he didn't worry about Ita then. He's just covering up the real reason he didn't admit to being here around the time that Cetterick was murdered.'

Flann turned courteously towards Bran, as if inviting him to answer, but Bran said nothing.

'Well?' said Flann. 'We're waiting for the real reason why you didn't mention this before.'

Bran faced him boldly. 'Could I speak to you in private, Master?' he asked.

Flann considered this and then shook his head. 'I think it wouldn't be right to exclude any of my students. You have all been involved in my murder inquiries before, and you all know that everything that is said as evidence is to be kept a secret among the members of the Drumshee law school. Rory had to give us his evidence in front of every one of my students; there is no reason why you should be treated differently, Bran. Anything you have to say now must be heard by all.'

Bran glanced at Ita with a little smile on his face. She scowled back; then, with a sudden lurch of her heart, she guessed what he was going to say.

'I didn't want to anger you, Master, by letting you know that I was thinking of becoming a Christian,' said Bran softly. 'You see, Ita and I . . . Well, I hope to make Ita my wife, and I wanted your good will before I asked your permission.'

Ita jumped forward, swinging her plaits back and facing her father. 'That's not true, Father!' she cried. 'He's lying. Nothing like that has ever been said between us. I don't even like him!'

'That's true,' said Cathal eagerly. 'She can't stand him!'

'Shut up,' said Ita ungratefully. 'I can speak for myself. Father, I assure you, there's never been any mention of anything like that. Go on, Bran, tell him! Did you ever speak to me about marriage?'

'Well, not in so many words,' said Bran, looking at her indulgently. 'But you knew, didn't you, that I admired you – that I loved you? I must have shown it a thousand times every day.'

'Go away!' shouted Ita. To her horror, she felt tears come to her eyes and pour down her cheeks.

'I think,' said Flann, 'that everyone is tired, and that we should go home and leave this discussion for the morning. We will be burying Cetterick, and King Carthen will be coming for the ceremony.'

'Do you want to ride back with me, Ita?' asked Fergal in an undertone, as everyone moved to untie the ponies from the nearby trees. 'Or would you prefer to ride with your father?'

'I'd rather go with you,' said Ita hurriedly. 'Quick, let's go now – fast. I want to get away from that stupid pig Bran. I'll kill him if he says another word to me – and I don't care what sort of fine I'd have to pay, either.'

'A pig has no honour-price,' said Fergal, a smile lighting up his small dark face. 'Don't worry,' he added, 'your father doesn't believe him. You know what the Brehon is like; he's playing with him like a cat with a mouse. He knows you love Mahon; we all know that. You'll be getting married soon, I suppose.'

'I don't know,' said Ita drearily. 'I don't know what

Mahon wants. I don't know what I want, either. Everything seems to be going wrong these days. I wish Bran had never come here . . . Do you think he could have murdered Cetterick, Fergal?'

'I can't see why, can you?' said Fergal. 'Anyway, maybe after this the Brehon will get rid of him. If I were you, I would tell your father that Bran keeps pestering you.'

'That seems mean,' said Ita uneasily. 'I've never done that sort of thing – not since I was about six years old. I remember complaining to him about Cathal pulling my plaits. Mind you, he only did it after I called him Carrot-Head because he wouldn't let me score a goal at hurley.' She smiled as she remembered the scene. 'My father told me then that I'd have to fight my own battles if I wanted to be in the law school; and being a law-school scholar was the most important thing in the world to me then.'

And it still is, she thought, as she rode beside Fergal. She could see him looking anxiously at her from time to time. She took a deep breath and smiled at him.

'Don't worry about me, Fergal,' she said. 'I'm fine. The important thing now is Cetterick's murder. We'll need to forget about everything else and concentrate on finding out the truth.'

# Chapter 8

Cetterick was to be buried outside his church. The king had decreed that. Flann and his scholars were there an hour before the ceremony; everything had to be ready before the king's arrival. A team of four men, taking turns, two by two, were still digging the grave when they arrived.

'Look,' whispered Aidan, nodding towards a man leaning on a spade. 'That's Oisín. I wonder if he'll get the land back now, or if the king will put another priest here. There aren't many Christians left – only three or four.'

Ita looked with interest at Oisín. She knew him, but hadn't seen him for a long time. He was a well-built young man with dark, intense eyes and very black hair and beard.

'He looks happy, doesn't he?' she said in an undertone to Fergal.

'That's the girl he's going to marry,' Fergal whispered in her ear. 'The one over beside the church door. Her name is Aoife and she's from Liscannor.'

Ita would have guessed even if Fergal hadn't spoken: Oisín's eyes were fixed fondly on the small, pretty girl with soft light-brown plaits. Ita liked the look of Aoife. She hoped that they would be happy, and that Oisín would get his land back from the king so he and Aoife could get married immediately and have enough to live on. *That's if he had nothing to do with the murder*, she told herself.

The night before, she had lain awake for a long time. She had decided to put her worries about Bran and Mahon and Mara and Britus out of her head, and to concentrate on helping her father find the murderer. *The rule of law must prevail*, she said sternly to herself. Oisín certainly didn't look as if he mourned Cetterick's death – but then, neither did anyone else. Everyone seemed to be joking and talking and enjoying the sunshine of the late-summer day.

Suddenly Ita thought of something. She moved over to her father. 'Father,' she said in a whisper, 'shouldn't Mara and her mother be here?'

'The king did not wish it,' said Flann quietly. 'In life Cetterick rejected them; in death he might not welcome them.'

Poor Mara, thought Ita, returning to her place beside Fergal. *Imagine not having a father who thought you were wonderful in every way!* Suddenly a feeling of pity overcame her dislike for Mara. *After all*, she thought, *she can't help looking gorgeous and having all the boys fall in love with her.* Even Bran, she thought with a glance of dislike – which he answered with a smirk – was attracted to Mara.

The solemn music began. Finbar, looking much older than he had when he left to join the king at his court, was playing a lament on his horn. Nessa, his young wife, stood in the background, holding a small baby. Nessa looked years older, too, thought Ita. Once they had been friends, equals; now Nessa was a woman with her hair bound up in linen, while Ita was still a scholar – still a 'girl in plaits', as the law texts put it.

The burial service was short; many people were there, but it seemed as if they had come to honour the king rather than to honour the dead priest. Ita, looking around, could see no tears, no traces of mourning on any face. It seemed strange that no little bowls of food, no household goods were put into the grave with Cetterick's body; there was no eulogy, either, and no bard recorded the dead man's ancestors. Oisín, his job as gravedigger done, stood aside, but his eyes were not on the coffin: they were roaming over the land around the church. As soon as the body was consigned to the ground and he had helped the other gravediggers to shovel back the yellow earth, he approached Flann.

'My lord,' he said in a low voice, 'would this be a good time to talk to the king about getting my land back? You know that Aoife and I —' He cast a proud, loving glance at the pretty girl waiting for him. 'You know that we are intending to get married. Those extra twenty acres would make a great difference to us. I don't suppose he'll be putting another priest here; there are too few Christians left — even my own *taoiseach* hardly goes near the church these days.'

'Come to my house in an hour,' said Flann. 'The king has just told me that he will honour my house with a visit.' He turned to Ita. 'Tell one of the boys to ride ahead and give notice to Fionnuala that the king will be with us for the midday meal.'

'I'll go,' said Ita rapidly. 'Fionnuala will work herself into a state if she hears that King Carthen is coming to our house.'

'I'll ride back with you,' said Fergal.

'We'll all go,' said Aidan. 'We'll keep Fionnuala so busy finding us all work to do that she won't have time to panic.'

'I'll ride with you and the king, Master,' said Bran.

'He would!' said Cathal, as soon as they had ridden

a few paces ahead. 'He'll be trying to impress the king with how clever he is.'

'It might work, too,' said Ninian thoughtfully. 'The king never strikes me as . . .' He lowered his voice, with a quick glance over his shoulder. 'King Carthen never strikes me as being very intelligent. He knows absolutely no law.'

'So he mightn't realise how stupid Bran is and how very intelligent the rest of us are,' said Ita with a smile.

'I could not have put it better myself,' said Ninian, with a very good imitation of Flann's judicious manner.

There was a delicious smell of roast venison coming from the kitchen-house when they entered the enclosure at Drumshee. Ita breathed a sigh of relief. Malachy and his friends had been hunting deer in the forest beyond Kylemore all this week, and they had given presents of venison to all their neighbours; there would be plenty of meat.

Fionnuala was bustling around the kitchen preparing vegetables. 'The king will love this, Fionnuala,' Ita said calmly. 'It's nice that you won't be wasting all this cooking on me and the boys – you know what my father is like; he never notices what he eats.'

'The king!' Fionnuala gave a shriek of alarm, but a quick glance around the kitchen calmed her: this was going to be a meal fit for a king.

'Donogh,' she shouted at her half-deaf husband, 'get out the mead and the silver goblets. Diarmuid and Fergal, you take the table out of the Brehon's room, carry it out into the yard and sweep that room – properly, mind you! Aidan and Cathal, you go down to the big meadow and gather some meadowsweet to strew on the floor when it's been swept. Ninian, you'd better go with them and stop them larking around. Ita, get out the linen tablecloth and the silver bowl, for the king to wash his hands in – oh, and the silver candlesticks. And use new candles in them, Ita – beeswax candles, not the goose-fat ones . . .'

Everyone leaped into action. By the time Flann, Owen, Bran and King Carthen arrived, the meal was ready and the biggest room of the Brehon's house was shining with cleanliness, fragrant with the almond-smell of freshly gathered meadowsweet and gleaming with polished silver.

The seven scholars served the king, Flann and Owen, and then happily cleared away the remains of the meal when they had finished.

'Great!' said Aidan. 'Look how much they've left. We can stuff ourselves!'

'Have all you like,' beamed Fionnuala. The king had sent congratulations to her and she was in high good humour. 'I don't suppose he gets better meals than that in his own place,' she said proudly.

The scholars had just finished eating and were helping Fionnuala to clean up when Oisín came into the enclosure, looking nervous and determined. Diarmuid went across to tell Flann; he came back with the message that the king would see Oisín in a quarter of an hour, in the schoolhouse, and that all the scholars were to be present.

'He'll be in a good mood,' said Fergal reassuringly. 'I poured a second jug of mead when I was in there last, and he had most of the first jug – Owen only had one goblet, and the Brehon has hardly touched his.'

Oisín nodded. He didn't smile, though, and his eyes were fixed on the candle-clock that Fionnuala kept in the kitchen to time her cooking. As soon as the flame had reached the quarter-mark he jumped to his feet, cleared his throat and looked at Diarmuid.

'I'll show you the way,' said Diarmuid, cramming his mouth with a last piece of deliciously crusty venison and then wiping it quickly with the sleeve of his tunic.

'Make sure you are tidy, all of you!' called out Fionnuala, but no one cared. They had all had a few drops of mead in their dewberry cordial and they felt very merry indeed. They crowded into the schoolhouse, elbowing and giggling. Aidan set out a stool in a corner and turned to Bran with a low bow: 'For you, my lord,' he said politely. Then all the others picked up their stools and, sniggering wildly, sat down on the other side of the room, as far from Bran as they could get. He coloured up angrily, but at that moment footsteps sounded on the flagstones outside, so he didn't attempt to move. The other six straightened their faces hurriedly, and they all rose solemnly to their feet as the king entered.

'Sit down, sit down,' King Carthen said genially. Fergal was right: he did seem to be in a good mood. He sat down on Flann's chair and leaned back. His stomach looked even larger than it had a couple of hours earlier, thought Ita. Flann, neat and unobtrusive as ever, took Owen's chair and sat beside him; Owen sat at the end of the table, on one of the stools.

The king smiled around at everyone. 'So, Oisín, you have a petition to make to me,' he boomed. 'Let me hear it, then.'

'My lord,' said Oisín nervously, 'I am shortly to be

married, and my clan can only spare ten acres of land for me. I was wondering if I could have back those twenty acres that were given to the priest – now that he's dead. Those twenty acres were meant to go to me whenever I got married.'

The king's smile vanished. 'They will be needed for another priest,' he said shortly.

'My lord,' cried Oisín, desperation lending a rough note to his voice, 'it's not worth your while sending another priest here. No one of importance around here is still a Christian.'

'*I* am a Christian,' stated the king, and the cold note in his voice made Ita look at Oisín with sympathy.

'Yes, but, my lord,' Oisín stumbled on, 'no one here wants to be a Christian now. They all hated Cetterick so much that they wanted nothing to do with his religion.'

There was a long, cold silence. King Carthen stared at Oisín. His face was like stone, and when he spoke his voice was as hard and as cold. He didn't speak to Oisín; he turned and faced Flann.

'Have you questioned this man yet about Cetterick's death?'

'No, my lord,' replied Flann.

'Well, do so now, in my presence.'

Flann nodded. His face showed no emotion. He turned to Oisín.

'You knew Cetterick,' he stated.

Oisín nodded.

'When did you last see him?'

Oisín hesitated; then he said defiantly, 'Yesterday morning. The morning that he was killed.'

'And what time in the morning?' asked Flann mildly.

'About an hour or so before noon.'

A ripple of excitement went through the students.

'Where was he when you saw him?'

'In the church,' said Oisín.

'And he was alive?'

'Oh, he was alive all right,' said Oisín bitterly. 'He was kicking that unfortunate slave boy of his.'

'And you went into the church to talk to Cetterick.'

'Yes, I did,' said Oisín. He stopped, looking at the king. 'You see, my lord,' he said appealingly, 'that land has got into a terrible state. Cetterick was allowing gorse bushes to grow all over it. Have you seen it?' he demanded passionately. 'Have you seen the land around the church? You can't even see the old burial mound now; it's completely overgrown with gorse. I went into the church – I knew Cetterick was in there; I could hear him screaming at Britus. I went in to . . . to ask him to at least look after the land. I even offered to cut down the gorse myself and burn the land to clean it.'

'I suppose you thought you might get the land back, in one way or another,' said the king scornfully.

Oisín straightened his back and said with dignity, 'I thought it was possible, my lord, seeing how few people were still coming to the church.'

Fergal whispered in Ita's ear, 'He's a tough character, this Oisín,' and then hastily turned his head away as he saw Flann looking at him.

Oisín was tough, Ita thought; he was determined. And, of course, he was very much in love. And he was probably tougher than Rory, who was a gentle giant unless he had drink taken . . .

'And what did Cetterick say to you?' asked Flann.

'Oh, he just screamed at me. He told me to get out and not to show my face inside his church again. I saw it was no use talking to him, so I left. As I shut the door behind me, I heard that poor boy scream. I was going to go back, but I thought that might just make things worse for Britus, so I went off.'

'Did you go back to your own house?' asked Flann.

Again Oisín hesitated, but then he drew a deep

breath and looked Flann in the eyes. 'No, my lord,' he said. 'I went up to the hill behind the church. I wanted to see how bad the problem with the gorse was getting up there.'

'Could you see the church? Did you see anyone go in or come out?'

'Yes, my lord,' said Oisín readily. 'I saw a girl go in – a beautiful girl with masses of golden hair. And then, after a while, I saw Britus come out. He went across towards Lough Fergus. He's helping young Mahon with the house he's building down there.'

'And did you see anything else?'

'I went home shortly after that,' said Oisín. His tone was evasive. Ita saw Ninian raise his eyebrows and look at Flann.

Flann waited for a minute and then, quietly and patiently, repeated his question: 'And did you see anything else?'

'This man is avoiding your questions,' interrupted King Carthen angrily. 'He sounds guilty to me. I think he should stand trial as the killer – the secret killer – of Cetterick the priest.'

Oisín's dark-skinned face flushed suddenly, and a look of panic came into his eyes. *He's thinking of Aoife,* thought Ita with ready sympathy; *he's thinking of his marriage, the happy life he's hoping to lead. The land suddenly doesn't seem so important to him; life is more important than any land . . .*

Oisín was staring intently at Flann, and his struggle to make up his mind was clear on his face. Suddenly he smashed his fist down on the table. 'Yes, I did,' he said loudly. 'I saw the girl come out after Britus had gone. She went over to the well outside the church. I could see her very clearly — in fact, I moved down the hill to get a good look at her — and I could see what she was doing.'

'And what was she doing?' asked Flann quietly.

'She was washing her hands,' said Oisín. 'She was . . .' He stopped, looking shamefaced and reluctant; but then his eyes hardened. *He's remembering the danger he's in himself*, thought Ita.

'She was washing her hands,' he repeated defiantly. 'There was blood all over her hands.'

'Did she see you?' asked Flann.

'No,' said Oisín slowly. 'She just walked away. I didn't speak to her. I didn't go into the church. I didn't want to know what had happened. I just went home.'

'There's a sundial beside the church door,' said Flann. 'Cetterick had it there so that people could know when the church services would begin. Did you look at it?'

Oisín nodded. 'Yes, my lord. The shadow showed it was just after eleven o'clock.'

'And was this after you had seen the girl?'

'Yes, my lord,' said Oisín gravely. 'It was after I had seen her wash blood from her hands.'

 # Chapter 9

'It couldn't have been Mara!' exclaimed Diarmuid. He hadn't had an opportunity to say anything before – Flann had kept busy bidding a ceremonial farewell to the king – and by now he sounded ready to explode.

'Why not?' said Ita sourly. 'You saw for yourself: I was able to lift that candlestick and bring it down on the gorse bush. Why not Mara?'

'Yes, but a girl like that!' cried Diarmuid.

'You sound like Bran. You're not giving any reasons; you're saying it couldn't have been Mara just because she's pretty,' retorted Ita, with a hasty glance over her shoulder at the schoolhouse, where her father was talking to Bran. She couldn't bear the thought that they might be talking about her.

'Ita's right,' said Ninian. 'We have to look at the evidence. If Oisín is telling the truth, then Mara will have to explain what she was doing washing blood off her hands just after eleven, when she told us that her father was still alive at that time.'

'I'm not saying that she did it,' said Ita hastily. 'I'm

just saying that it's not impossible.'

'What about Oisín?' asked Fergal. 'He could have done it. He was there; he admitted it himself. And he admitted that he was furiously angry with Cetterick.'

'And he could have said that about Mara just to turn suspicion away from himself,' said Diarmuid eagerly.

'That's what the king thought, isn't it?' said Aidan. '"I don't believe this man, do you, Brehon?"' he boomed, pinching his nose to imitate King Carthen's nasal tone.

'I think the master was inclined to believe Oisín, though,' said Ninian.

'I thought so, too,' said Ita. 'Something about the way he was looking at Oisín . . . It's very hard to tell with him, though.'

'Now, off to bed with you all,' said Fionnuala, appearing at the kitchen-house door. 'You're keeping Ita up, and she's looking very tired.'

'No, I'm not,' said Ita; but, in fact, she was feeling rather miserable. She tucked her hand into Fionnuala's arm and allowed herself to be led away. It was nice to have Fionnuala come over to the Brehon's house with her, wash her hair in lavender-scented water and comb it dry in front of the fire.

'I'll wear my new tunic tomorrow, Fionnuala,' she

said sleepily as she slid down under her warm lambskin cover. 'My father says we're all going to ride over to Inchicronan Lake to see Mara and Britus – and Mara's mother, I suppose,' she added, suddenly remembering this woman cast aside by a man who wanted to be a priest, not a husband and a father.

'You can wear that nice coloured belt that your father bought you at Kinvara,' said Fionnuala, bustling over to the chest to pull out all Ita's best clothes. 'And your gold brooch; I'll fasten it onto your cloak for you. I'll come over to comb your hair and do your plaits, and we'll put on your gold-embroidered headband. Don't worry, you'll be prettier than that Mara. She looks as if that hair of hers never saw a comb!'

Ita smiled into her pillow. Fionnuala would never admit that Mara's cloud of red-gold hair was the prettiest thing she had ever seen. She felt drowsy and happy after her bath.

Then the voice of Bran bidding her father good night roused her. She sat up in bed, but then she lay down quickly and shut her eyes. She didn't want to talk about Bran, or about anyone else, she decided; if her father came into her room, she would pretend to be asleep. But he didn't come.

Somewhat to her surprise, Ita slept well and woke

up feeling more cheerful. Breakfast was quick, and the sundial in the yard only pointed to nine o'clock when they all mounted their ponies and followed Flann down the lane from Drumshee.

It was about an hour before they all, led by Owen, galloped into the farmyard near Lake Inchicronan. Although it was still early, there were two visitors there before them. One was Mahon, who was busily mending the roof of a hen-house, with Mara watching him; the other was Donal the physician, holding his horse by the bridle and engaged in deep conversation with a woman. *That must be Mara's mother*, thought Ita, trying to ignore Mahon, who had blushed a deep red at the sight of her, and Fergal, who was giving her a concerned glance. Yes, the woman was definitely Mara's mother: despite the fact that her hair was turning grey and there were deep lines of sorrow around her mouth, she still had traces of Mara's beauty.

'Well, Donal,' said Flann.

'Brehon,' Donal said curtly. He opened his mouth as if to explain his presence, then shut it with a defiant look. He mounted his horse heavily.

'I'm off,' he said, with a quick nod to the woman and a glance across at Mara.

Flann stared after him thoughtfully. Then he

turned and bowed, with his usual courtesy, to the woman.

'I am Flann the Brehon,' he said. 'I have met your daughter.'

'And my husband, Cetterick,' said the woman harshly.

Flann bowed again, but said nothing. There was a moment's tense silence. Mara crossed the yard to her mother's side; Mahon slid down from the hen-house roof and came to stand shoulder to shoulder with Mara. Ita looked across at the distant lake. To her horror, she felt tears well up in her eyes.

'My name is Grana,' said the woman, breaking the silence abruptly.

'These are my students,' said Flann. 'You may speak in front of them; they are all trained to keep silence, outside the law school, about any law affair. I have a few questions for you, and then I wish to speak to your daughter Mara and to the slave boy Britus.'

At the sound of his name, Britus came out of the house. He still looked scared and thin, but his colour was better, Ita was glad to see; Mara and her mother must have been kind to him. He stood silently behind Mara, and she gave him a reassuring glance over her shoulder.

'Ask and be done with it,' said Grana. 'We have work to do.'

'How long have you been separated from your husband?' asked Flann.

'About eighteen months,' said Grana. Her tone was indifferent, almost careless.

'You were separated, or divorced?'

Ninian took a quick step forward. His keen, clever eyes moved quickly from Flann to Grana.

'Separated,' said Grana firmly. 'Cetterick, as a Christian, didn't believe in divorce, and I didn't ask for one. I hoped he would come to his senses and return to his wife and family.'

'And when did you last see him?'

'Not since he left me,' replied Grana.

'And you sent your daughter to see him two days ago?'

Grana shook her head. 'That was her own idea,' she said. 'I told her not to go. There was no point in going; Cetterick wasn't a man to be swayed easily.'

Flann nodded. His eyes went to Mara and then returned to her mother.

'A man of violence, would you say?' he asked gently.

'A man of violence,' agreed Grana, without heat; she sounded almost bored. She turned as if to walk away.

'And you know Donal the physician?' asked Flann rapidly.

The question clearly disconcerted her. Suddenly her face was alive and almost frightened, as if a sudden and unwelcome thought had struck her.

'He is my brother,' she said after a long minute.

'And he knew how much you had suffered?'

Grana shrugged. The mask of indifference came down over her face again. 'I keep my sufferings to myself,' she said firmly. 'I don't complain – not to my brother, not to my daughter.'

Flann gazed at her intently; then he turned to Mara. 'Your father was alive when you left him?' he asked.

'Yes, my lord,' said Mara confidently.

'I think you told us that was nearly an hour before noon?'

'Yes, my lord,' repeated Mara. Ita thought there was a hint of mockery in the repeated 'my lord', but it was impossible to be sure. Mara's beautiful face was deferential, her brilliant green eyes wide and innocent.

'You knew the time by the shadow on the sundial, I suppose,' mused Flann casually. Fergal, Ita noticed, shot his master a quick glance, and so did Ninian;

they all knew that tone of voice. Mara, however, sensed no threat.

'Yes, my lord,' she said confidently. 'The sun was very bright that morning.'

'And why did you have blood on your hands if your father was still alive?' asked Flann. The question came out rapidly, but his voice was still calm and quiet.

Mara and Grana both started. Mahon put a protective hand on Mara's shoulder, but she shrugged it off. For a moment her gold-tipped black eyelashes swept down over the wild-rose flush of her cheeks; then she raised them and looked straight at Flann, with big, puzzled eyes.

'I had no blood on my hands, my lord,' she said.

'Someone saw you,' said Flann. 'Someone saw you go to the well and wash the blood from your hands.'

'Ah!' There was a soft intake of breath, a short pause, and then Mara smiled.

'When I pleaded with my father, my lord,' she said, slowly and carefully, 'I took his hands in mine. After he threw me off, I washed the feel of his hands away. I went to the well and washed my hands of him.'

'And yet our witness says that he saw blood on your hands – saw it plainly,' said Flann.

'He is mistaken, my lord,' said Mara firmly. She smiled innocently. 'The sun was bright that day; it was probably in his eyes.'

'I see,' said Flann. 'And when you came back, when you found Cetterick dead, was the body already on the altar?'

Britus made a sound, something between a gasp and a groan, and Flann whirled around to look at him. Ita kept her eyes fixed on Mara; for a moment she could have sworn some hint of astonishment came into the girl's strange green eyes, but when she spoke, her voice was clear and confident as always.

'Yes, my lord,' she said.

'So you can add nothing to your story about the death of your father Cetterick.'

'Nothing, my lord,' said Mara firmly.

Flann looked at her for a long moment, but she was silent. He turned to Britus.

'When you left your master Cetterick with his daughter, what did you do next?'

Britus stared at him, panic-stricken.

'He went straight over to do his work with Mahon, my lord,' said Mara helpfully.

'I'd prefer him to answer for himself,' said Flann gently. 'Perhaps, Mahon, you might like to go back to your work on the roof – and Mara, you might want to go on assisting him.'

Mara opened her mouth – to protest, probably; but Mahon was used to obeying Flann without question, and he was already moving back towards the hen-house. Mara, after a moment's hesitation and a quick squeeze of Britus's hand, followed him.

'Well?' said Flann. 'Did you go straight to Mahon's house, or did you wait outside the church to see what was happening?'

Britus looked around helplessly. Ita turned sharply, and just caught Mara nodding her head.

'Yes,' muttered the boy.

'You waited outside?'

This time Mara shook her head.

'No,' said Britus, with a look at her. 'I went away.'

'And your master was still alive then?'

Another quick, furtive glance at Mara, and this time there was no doubt: Ita saw Mara nod encouragingly. This time Flann noticed, as well. He hardly listened to Britus's muttered, 'Yes.' Frowning heavily, he took the boy by the arm.

'Come with me, Britus,' he said with calm authority. 'We'll go outside the gate. No, don't worry; I won't hurt you in any way. Owen, you come with me; the rest of you, stay here.'

After the three left the farmyard enclosure and

walked towards the lake, there was complete silence. Mahon gave up any pretence of mending the hen-house roof and climbed back down; his eyes, concerned and loving, were fixed on Mara. It was hard to read Mara's face. She gazed after Britus, her green eyes thoughtful; then, suddenly, she turned and went into the house. A minute later she came out of the back door and disappeared behind a clump of bushes.

'She's going to creep after them and listen,' whispered Aidan, his eyes full of admiration. *It doesn't seem to matter what Mara does*, thought Ita bitterly; *all the boys just think she's wonderful.*

She glanced at Mahon and saw him looking back at her. His face was flushed and tense, as if he was making up his mind to do something difficult. Resolutely he crossed the yard and stood in front of her.

'Could I speak to you in private for a minute?' he asked abruptly. He turned and walked back towards the hen-house.

Ita followed him reluctantly. Suddenly she knew what he wanted to say. It made no difference to him that she was wearing her best cloak and her prized gold brooch; that her hair shone from Fionnuala's vigorous brushing, that her gold-embroidered hair-band was bound around her head. Mahon had eyes for only one beauty now.

'Ita,' he said, and he said it with a gasp as if he had just plunged into ice-cold water. 'Ita, I have to be honest with you. I love Mara, and I want to marry her. I'll always be fond of you, but it's more like . . . like the way I would be fond of a sister. I want to marry Mara – and she wants to marry me.' He seemed dazzled by his own good fortune. 'We talked to her mother last night, and she's willing for us to be married as soon as the house is built.'

Ita gazed at him. She couldn't say anything; the lump in her throat was too big, too painful. Her hands felt cold and her legs were trembling.

She turned and walked back across the yard. It seemed a long, long way. There had been times during the last few months when she had wondered whether she and Mahon were really suited to each other, but now she felt as if she had lost something very precious. She sat on the wall by the gate and stared with hot, unseeing eyes at her father and Owen and Britus standing near the lake. It was only when she blinked away a couple of tears that she noticed that Mara had crept up, concealed by a clump of bushes, quite close to where they were standing.

What do I care? Ita thought numbly, turning away. *I don't care about anything. This is the worst day of my life.*

 # Chapter 10

'She was listening, of course,' said Aidan, kicking his heels into the sides of his fat pony in a vain effort to make it go faster.

'And signalling to Britus,' said Cathal. 'Every time the Brehon asked him a question, she signalled the answer. I could see her nodding or shaking her head.'

'That was an interesting question the Brehon asked Mara,' said Fergal thoughtfully. 'I mean about whether she found the body on the altar. You'd expect him to ask, "Was he dead when you arrived back?" not, "Was he already on the altar?"'

'Almost as if he thinks one person murdered Cetterick and another put him on the altar,' said Ita. Despite herself, she began to get interested. 'Father,' she called.

Flann was riding ahead, deep in conversation with Owen, but at the sound of her voice he immediately reined in his horse and turned around. His keen eyes scrutinised Ita intently, and she felt herself flushing. *He's guessed that something happened*, she thought, and began to speak rapidly in order to distract him.

'Father, Fergal and I were discussing the question you asked Mara, about whether the body was already on the altar when she went into the church the second time. We wondered whether you thought Cetterick was killed by one person and then put on the altar by another.'

'I think it's possible,' agreed Flann gravely.

Ita hesitated and then went on: 'Father, did you notice a piece of wood that was lying on the floor beside the altar? I've only just remembered it – I saw it when Fergal and I found the body. It looked like – like the end of one of the yew wands that Rua uses to find answers to questions.'

'I hadn't noticed that,' said Flann, slowly and heavily. All the other students looked at Ita with interest.

Again she hesitated. She knew how much her father revered Rua. *The law is there to find the truth,* she repeated in her mind; aloud she said, 'Could it have been Rua who put the body on the altar? Maybe he went to the church with the wands. He might have wanted to perform some ceremony there – maybe some spell to make Cetterick go away . . .'

'It's possible,' agreed Flann.

'Could it have been Rua who killed him, Master?' asked Diarmuid. He asked it humbly and carefully, but Flann showed no signs of anger.

'We must keep every possibility in mind,' he said, and rode on. Within moments he was deep in conversation with Owen again.

'Yes!' exclaimed Diarmuid. 'I knew it was Rua.'

'You're forgetting Oisín's evidence,' pointed out Ita. She was conscious that a cold, hard feeling of anger possessed her. Why was it that all the boys were determined to forget the evidence about Mara? 'He saw Mara come out of the church and wash blood off her hands.'

'I think Ita's right,' said Bran enthusiastically. 'Mara murdered Cetterick – Mahon probably helped her,' he added.

'How could he? He didn't even know her,' said Ninian scornfully.

'That's right,' said Cathal. 'The first time Mahon saw Mara was that time in the schoolhouse. That was obvious to anyone who looked at his face. He looked as if he'd been struck by lightning – sorry, Ita, but that was the way he looked,' he added uncomfortably.

Ita flushed a painful red, but Fergal spoke first. 'Anyway, Bran, I thought you were so sure Britus did it,' he said scornfully. 'Why have you suddenly changed your mind?'

'Ita convinced me,' said Bran, with a sweet smile at Ita. She ignored him and turned to Fergal.

'Do you think it was Mara?' she asked.

Fergal's eyes were troubled. 'If Mara did do it,' he said quietly, 'Christian law will want her dead – hanged as a murderer. Under Brehon law, she'll be guilty of *fingal*, killing a member of her family – the worst crime of all – and the punishment for that is to be put out to sea in a boat without oars, and left to die of thirst or drowning.'

Suddenly Ita felt sick with shame. She had been thinking that, if only Mara were out of the way, Mahon would come back to her. Fergal's words made her realise that she didn't want Mara to die – just to go away. She wanted everything to be as if Mara, with her beautiful face and her glorious gold hair, had never come to Drumshee. She couldn't answer Fergal; she couldn't even look at him. Quickly she kicked her pony and caught up with her father. She was conscious that he and Owen went on talking, discussing the case, but nothing they said made any sense to her. Her thoughts went around and around in circles, like a trapped marten-cat in a cage.

'We're going over to see Rua the druid,' said Flann, laying a warm hand on her cold one. 'Would you like to go home and get Fionnuala to make you a hot drink? You don't look very well.'

'I'm all right,' said Ita, avoiding his concerned eyes.

Her father nodded. For a moment she thought he was going to say something. Owen, with his usual sensitivity, had fallen back to join the other lads, leaving her alone with Flann. Ita wanted to beg her father to talk to Mahon, make him see sense; but she knew this was one problem she would have to solve for herself.

I'll ride over to Lough Fergus tomorrow and talk to him, she thought. *If Mara isn't around, he might remember everything he felt for me before* ... The thought made her feel a bit more cheerful. Perhaps Fionnuala was right, and it was just novelty that made Mahon love Mara. Perhaps she and her mother would go away, and then Mahon would forget all about the beautiful girl with the golden hair.

'Do you think the king might do something for Mara and her mother?' she asked her father, in a carefully unconcerned tone. 'After all, he was responsible for Cetterick abandoning them and leaving them so poor. Do you think he might give them land somewhere – wherever they came from originally?'

'I'll certainly mention the subject to him,' said Flann gravely, and Ita felt a slight prick of hope. *Mahon might forget Mara if she moved far away*, she thought.

'Let's get on,' she shouted over her shoulder, setting a fast pace on her pony and hearing the others thunder after her. 'Come on, Aidan!' she called. 'Bet Primrose can beat that fat pony of yours.'

'Don't insult my Podgy!' Aidan called back in mock anger. 'Anyway, he's nowhere near as fat as Bran's poor beast. At least Podgy gets exercised.'

When they arrived at the little oak grove they all slowed down, awed by the sacred atmosphere. Rua was standing in front of his house, almost as if he had been expecting them.

'Greetings, Brehon,' he said gravely.

Flann dismounted from his horse and gave the bridle to Owen. He walked forward, bowed low, and then spoke swiftly.

'When I spoke to you last, Rua, you said: "When Donal had gone, I went in, and the sacrifice was laid on the altar-table."' Flann stopped, but Rua said nothing, just inclined his head slightly.

'I ask you now,' Flann went on, every word slow and measured, 'did you mean that Cetterick's body was already on the altar when you entered, or that you laid it there yourself?'

There was a pause. All the students were holding their breath. In the dead silence, a grey crow rose squawking from the trees beyond.

Then Rua spoke. 'I put the body on the altar,' he agreed. He turned and looked at the stone circle, and his voice was singsong and dreamy: 'But was it a sacrifice to my gods or to his?'

'And when did you go to the church?'

Rua hoisted an indifferent shoulder. 'Times mean nothing to me, Brehon,' he said. 'My life is lived by the seasons, not by the hours.'

'And you saw Donal the physician?' asked Flann. Ita gave a start. Of course, Rua had mentioned this before; but they had all assumed that this had been when Diarmuid summoned Donal to examine the body. Now she realised that, if Donal had been there around the time Rua moved the body, it must have been before she and Fergal ever came to the church.

'I saw Donal,' agreed Rua.

'And anyone else?'

Rua paused. For a moment Ita thought he would refuse to answer. But Flann waited — courteous, but utterly determined — and Rua's eyes fell before the Brehon's calm stare.

'I saw the wronged one,' he said abruptly. Then he

turned and went into his house, slamming the door behind him.

'The question is: who is the wronged one?' said Fergal, as they rode through the dark wood and out onto the bright path beyond.

'Oisín, I suppose,' said Ninian.

'Or Mara,' said Ita, keeping her voice light and unconcerned. 'She was badly wronged by Cetterick, and so was her mother. And so was Donal the physician,' she added, suddenly realising the full significance of Rua's words. 'After all, it was his sister and his niece who were abandoned and shamed by Cetterick. And now we know from Rua that he was there before we found the body.'

'Where was he when you went to ask him to go see the body, Diarmuid?' asked Ninian.

'At his house, at Ballinacurra,' said Diarmuid.

'Well, that's only a few minutes' ride from the church,' said Aidan eagerly.

Diarmuid suddenly reined in his pony so hard that it reared and backed into Cathal's. 'Mind out, you fool!' yelled Cathal; but Diarmuid took no notice.

'Master,' he said, his blue eyes wide with horror and fixed on Flann, 'I've just remembered. When I came through Donal's gate, he was in his yard, washing something in a bucket. He took it out of the bucket and hung it on a bush before he came over to me. And, Master, I remember what it was. It was a tunic.'

★ ★ ★

The whole way to Donal's house, Ita found herself hoping that the physician had killed Cetterick. She was glad to find that she didn't really want Mara to be the murderer. She couldn't wish the terrible penalty for *fingal* on anyone, not even someone who had stolen Mahon from her. Donal was no blood relation to Cetterick. If they had fought and Donal had killed him by accident – perhaps even to defend himself – then surely, she tried to convince herself, the king wouldn't want him hanged. A physician was a valuable member of the community; even the Church might not call for his blood. Anyway, there was no priest to call for the death penalty now, and the king would probably allow his Brehon to administer justice in his own way. Donal could pay a fine to his sister Grana, and afterwards she and Mara could go away and live in comfort.

When Flann asked him about the tunic he had been washing, however, Donal calmly denied having any knowledge of Cetterick's murder.

'I went to see a child at Ballagh who had cut his arm on the iron shoe of a plough, Brehon,' he said

116

confidently. 'I got some blood on my tunic. I rinsed it out myself; old Macha, my housekeeper, was out, and I knew it would stain if it wasn't washed immediately.'

Flann nodded, got on his horse and made as if to ride away; after two strides, he reined in his horse. 'And Cetterick was dead when you looked into the church on your way back from Ballagh,' he said, so suddenly that even his students, used to his methods, were startled.

Donal wasn't taken off guard, though. 'I didn't go into the church, Brehon,' he said calmly. 'Not until you sent your lad here to get me.'

'And yet we have a witness who says you were there,' said Flann mildly.

'The Brehon's trying to trap him,' Fergal whispered in Ita's ear. 'Rua didn't actually say that Donal went into the church.'

'He's mistaken,' said Donal confidently. He thought for a moment and then said, 'But I did stop by the church door and get off my horse to look at the sundial. I wanted to check the time. I'm still not used to this place; I can't tell the time by the sun as easily as I could when I lived in Moy. It was about a quarter of an hour before noon.'

★ ★ ★

The whole of that evening, Ita, Diarmuid, Aidan, Cathal, Ninian and Fergal – keeping well away from Bran, who was following Owen around as usual – sat by the side of the River Fergus and went over and over the evidence.

Was Donal telling the truth when he said he had only stopped to look at the sundial? Or had Donal gone into the church and killed Cetterick? Perhaps he had been sent there by Mara, his sister's child; perhaps he had witnessed Cetterick's violence towards Mara.

And what about Oisín? Had he finally cracked and murdered the man who had taken, and ruined, the land the clan would have given to him and his bride?

And Rory? Fear of death by hanging might have made him kill Cetterick. Without Cetterick around, King Carthen would be unlikely to care about Rory's killing of the coppersmith; and the Brehon laws would only make him pay a fine.

And what about Bran? What had he really been doing hanging around the church? None of the law students believed his story about wanting to become a Christian.

'And then there's the question of the missing gold plate and cup,' said Diarmuid. 'Could it have been a passing thief, someone from another kingdom?'

'I don't think the Brehon believes that,' said Ninian thoughtfully. 'Owen has checked: no one saw any strangers near the church or Lough Fergus.'

By the time Ita went to bed, her mind was boiling over with ideas. She was glad of that: it helped her not to think about Mahon. She would think about him the next day. She would set out early in the morning, not bothering about breakfast, and ride over to Lough Fergus to talk with him.

 # Chapter 11

The next morning, Ita was woken by the twittering of the swallows swooping in and out of the barn to feed their last brood of fledglings. She got up and dressed quietly. Holding her shoes in her hand, she crept out of the Brehon's house, carefully easing the door shut so as not to wake her father. She stole across the enclosure and took Primrose from the stable. Bran's pony was missing, she noticed; he must have got up early and gone for a ride.

It was a bright, sunny morning, with a strong wind blowing the taste of the sea to her lips. She galloped Primrose down the lane and set off down the Togher Road, which led to the bog and beyond it to Lough Fergus. For some reason she didn't want to go by the river, which was her usual route to Lough Fergus; it had too many happy memories of going for rides with Mahon, or thinking about Mahon.

Now, Ita acknowledged to herself, that was probably all over. She recalled the look on Mahon's face when he looked at Mara; he loved her more than he had ever loved Ita. She had lost him. There was no point in being angry; that would change nothing. She hesitated and almost turned back, but then she made herself go on. If she didn't talk to him now, she would always wonder what might have happened.

Ita was so deep in her thoughts that she didn't notice the weather had changed. As so often happens in the west of Ireland, the fine morning had suddenly clouded over; the wind from the west strengthened, and Ita had to hold her cloak closed with one hand as she rode. When she looked up at the sky she saw storm clouds, the colour of blackberries in milk, rolling in from the Atlantic.

Once again Ita hesitated, but she was more than halfway to Mahon's; she was actually in the townland of Kylemore. *I'll shelter in the church*, she thought. *There's going to be a heavy shower, but the weather might clear up after that.* Holding her cloak tightly around her, she urged Primrose on.

As she reached the little hill overlooking the church, the rain began to fall. It was no summer shower, though; sheets of heavy, cold water battered her, and she could hardly see as the pony struggled down the hill. By the time they reached the church door, Ita was soaked through. She tied Primrose to the rail on the east side of the church, where she would be sheltered from the rain; then, breathless and shivering, she reached up to the great iron latch.

To her horror, however, the church was locked. The king must have ordered it to be locked in case anything else was stolen from it. Ita didn't know what to do. There was no point in standing there with the westerly wind driving the rain in her face, though; she would have to look for shelter. Pulling her sodden hood half over her face, Ita ran towards the clump of gorse that grew thickly on the hillside above the church.

The gorse was broken and trampled in places, as if someone with heavy boots had broken a passage through it. Thankfully Ita followed the passage; its walls half-sheltered her from the wind sweeping in from the sea. Someone had definitely been here before her, she noticed: there were threads of purple wool on the spines of the gorse. She looked at them curiously. The colour was bright and fresh; the threads hadn't been there for long.

She rounded a gorse bush; in front of her the ground sloped sharply upwards, and burrowing into the slope was a dark hole. Suddenly she remembered Oisín talking to the king about the gorse choking the land he felt was his. She could hear his passionate voice: 'Have you seen the land around the church? You can't even see the old burial mound now; it's completely overgrown with gorse.' That was what he had said; and now Ita knew where she was. The burial mound, beneath its shroud of gorse, was in front of her; the dark hole led into its side.

Ita hesitated. A feeling of awe and fear swept over her. Some long-gone people had buried their dead here . . . She almost turned away, but at that moment the rain changed to icy lumps of hail; the blackberry-coloured sky seemed to split open, and, with a roar of thunder, a jagged spear of lightning crashed onto the hill, not far above where she stood.

Ita plunged into the entrance. Another bolt of lightning illuminated the passageway with a white, searing light. From behind her came the resinous smell of burning gorse. The passageway was quite short – only about six paces long – but a small chamber led off it; and in that chamber a candle was burning.

Then, quite suddenly, the candle was snuffed out, leaving a lingering smell of hot wax and scorched skin. Not soon enough, however: in that instant, Ita had seen the purple cloak, the shining blond hair.

'Bran,' she whispered.

Giving herself no time to think, she moved

forward, guided by his heavy, frightened breathing, and snatched the hot candle. Quickly, moving backwards away from him, she fumbled in her pouch. Her fingers touched the smooth iron of her tinderbox; she struck a light and held the tiny flame to the candle.

The rich purple of Bran's cloak reflected in the gold torc that he wore around his slim, tanned neck. He had rings on his fingers, too, Ita noticed, and he was wearing a new brooch, the gold setting off the red precious stones that studded it. And then she forgot Bran and gave a cry of shock and surprise.

All the way around the little chamber were shelves made from slabs of stone. On them stood ancient burial urns, the bones of the long-dead gleaming white from their murky depths. But there were other things on the shelves, as well: torcs, rings, brooches, bracelets, heaps of them – and among them lay a gold communion cup and plate, and a small silver chessman.

'You stole all these!' Ita could hardly force the words from her mouth.

Bran shrugged contemptuously. 'Stole some, found others. The ancient people buried their dead with the jewels they had worn when they were alive.'

Her eyes returned to the chess piece. 'You took

the chessman from my father's house.'

He shrugged again. He didn't seem to think it worth replying. A hot spurt of anger went through her. She was aware of her cloak dripping on the flagstoned floor and of her feet like two solid blocks of ice, but none of that seemed to matter. Her eyes went back to the gold cup and plate.

'You killed Cetterick for those!'

He smiled teasingly. 'It was a pleasure,' he said, with the silly exaggerated bow that had always annoyed her. She stared at him. Was he admitting to the killing? Was he mad – didn't he care what would happen to him? Or was he just looking for attention, as usual?

'We'll see what my father has to say about that,' she said abruptly, and turned to go out of the chamber.

In a flash he was next to her, knocking the candle from her hand; it went out as it fell. His arms were around her. For a moment she thought he was going to kiss her, and she was almost relieved when she realised that he was tying her arms behind her back with his leather belt. She struggled, but Bran was stronger than he looked. She tried to kick him; he caught her foot in his hand and knocked her to the ground. Ita fell heavily, hurting herself, but she wouldn't give him the satisfaction of crying out. She could hear him panting and feel his breath hot on her cheek.

And then, suddenly, she could see him. He hadn't lit the candle again, but a light was coming down the little passageway – not the white glare of lightning, but the warm orange light of a wood fire. The gorse on the mound was on fire. Ita could smell it even in the mould-filled closeness of the chamber.

'Let me go, Bran,' she said between her teeth.

He laughed. 'Not until you promise to marry me,' he said lightly.

'I wouldn't marry you if you were the last man on earth,' she said passionately.

He laughed again. 'You'll marry me all right,' he said contemptuously. 'You don't seem to realise: you're in my power. I can do anything I like with you. I want to marry a Brehon's daughter – your father's getting old; I'll be able to take over the law school from him soon. I have a marriage contract here – Owen gave it to me to study. Once you've signed this, your father will have to agree. I'll keep you here until sunset – Owen told me that no one can change their minds once the sun has set on their wedding day – and then we'll go home and break the good news. If you don't sign, I'll leave you tied up

126

here. No one will find you for weeks, months — maybe years. It's your choice.'

Ita froze. It was true: she was completely in his power. And, even if she did sign, he might still harm her . . .

'Light the candle,' she said, keeping her voice as steady as possible. 'Then we can talk properly.' She took a deep breath. She had to keep calm. Bran wasn't clever; surely she could find some way to trick him and escape . . . She braced herself as she watched the tiny flame of the candle leap up and then steady itself.

Bran turned to place the candle on the stone shelf behind him, and at that moment Ita exploded into action. In a second she had rolled over and was on her feet; then she was running, faster than she had known she could, through the entrance of the chamber and down the passageway. Her bound hands made her clumsy and threw her off balance. She heard Bran behind her and felt his hand on her cloak. She pulled away from him with all her strength; the sudden jerk almost strangled her, but then she felt the soft gold of her brooch give way, and the heavy, sodden folds of her cloak fell away from her and into his hands. She heard him stumble and trip, and in another second she was outside the burial mound.

The rain and the clean wind were a relief after the heavy, dead smell of mould within the tomb. Instinctively Ita turned away from the crackling flames of the gorse fire and plunged downhill. Another gorse bush stood in her way; she burrowed deep into it, ignoring the pain of the sharp thorns digging into her arms. She crouched there, desperately trying to slow down the rapid breathing that might betray her.

Bran had come to the door of the tomb. The orange light of the burning gorse lit up dark smears of mould on his white tunic and his purple cloak. He must have stumbled and fallen over Ita's cloak; that had given her the precious extra seconds to make her escape. He looked around, narrowing his eyes against the glare, and Ita was sure his gaze lingered on the gorse bush where she was hiding. His hand went to his pouch; when it came out again, she saw a gleam of silver. He had taken out his knife.

Wildly she looked behind her. Could she crawl out of the gorse bush, somehow get back to the church before he saw her, and escape on Primrose? His pony must be tethered somewhere else – she had seen no sign of it near the church . . . Cautiously she began to move; and then she stopped. Above the hissing of the rain on the church roof and the creaking of the ash tree beyond, she had definitely heard a shout.

'Ita!' And then again: 'Ita!'

The second time she heard the voice clearly, and recognised it. It was Fergal. She strained her ears; his shout came again, but there was no other voice with it. He was alone. Would he be able to overpower Bran in a struggle? Bran was older, taller, and he had a knife in his hand. Quickly Ita decided. Let Fergal talk to Bran. He knew nothing, and Bran wouldn't risk attacking him. She would keep trying to get back to her pony.

'Bran!' Fergal's voice was very near her now. 'Bran, what are you doing there? Have you seen Ita? Her pony was wandering loose on the road by the bog.'

So Primrose bolted when the lightning and thunder frightened her, thought Ita. *Did Fergal bring her with him, or is she back in Drumshee?*

'Are you deaf, Bran?' shouted Fergal. 'I asked if you've seen Ita!'

'I haven't seen her; she's probably back home in the Brehon's house by now, tucked up in bed.' Bran's voice was light and unconcerned. 'But I'll help you look for her, if you like. I'll just go and find my pony.'

Quickly he turned and ran, in the opposite

direction from Ita and Fergal. *He won't come back*, thought Ita, and changed her plan. After all, even if Bran did come back, she and Fergal were two against one; and both of them, like Bran, always kept knives in their pouches.

'Fergal!' she called, dragging herself through the gorse bush. 'Fergal, Bran is a liar and a thief and I think he killed Cetterick – the gold plate and cup and all the other things he stole are in there, in the old burial mound . . . Don't go after him!' she screamed as Fergal, after a bewildered stare, turned to follow Bran. 'Take me home – please, Fergal, take me home to my father . . .' To her shock and embarrassment, tears were pouring down her face; she felt herself shaking all over, and she knew it wasn't just from the cold.

Fergal put his arms around her, and Ita thought she would never forget how warm and comforting it felt. She could always trust Fergal to do the right thing. In a moment he had picked her up, holding her close, and begun running downhill towards the church.

'I've got Primrose,' he panted as he struggled along. 'That's why I came to look for you. I saw you go out earlier, and I thought you had gone to see Mahon . . . I was coming to meet you; I thought you might be . . . might be a bit upset. I found Primrose running loose, and I thought maybe the thunder had frightened her and she had thrown you somewhere along the way. I managed to catch hold of her bridle, and then I came to look for you.'

They had reached the church. Primrose and Fergal's pony were tied to the rail, fidgeting irritably in the rain. Fergal took out his knife and slashed the leather belt that Bran had tied around Ita's wrists; then he hoisted her onto Primrose. Her hands and arms felt stiff and cramped, and she sat on Primrose's broad back turning her hands around and around and letting the rain drip from them. She was still shaking, and the tears continued to pour down her face. She was aware of Fergal giving her a worried look; she tried to manage a smile, but her lips puckered and trembled.

'I'd better get you back to your father,' he said. 'I hate to let Bran get away with this, though . . . Listen! Did you hear something? Someone's coming.'

'You young scholars are out in terrible weather! Why don't you stay tucked up in your nice warm schoolhouse? The only people who should be out on a day like this are working men like me,' said a voice.

The man's face was almost covered by the hood of his cloak, but his voice was familiar. Fergal shouted,

'Rory, did you see Bran?'

'The blond fellow? Yes, he's just galloped over that way, by the bog road.'

'Let's go after him!' shouted Fergal. 'He's . . . he stole some things, and he hurt Ita, and we think he killed Cetterick!'

Rory was a man of action; he shot off instantly, galloping towards the bog road. Fergal jumped on his own pony and then stopped.

'Will you be all right on your own for a moment, Ita? It won't take us long to catch him. Bran's pony is very fat – he doesn't exercise it much.'

'You go,' said Ita steadily. 'I'm fine.'

Fergal shot off. Ita hesitated for a moment, then followed him. She was still very shaken, and she didn't want to stay on her own. Suddenly the world seemed to be a dangerous place. After what had happened with Bran, she thought she would never feel safe again unless she was with her father, or with Fergal.

And I want to see Bran brought to justice, she thought as she urged Primrose on behind Fergal's pony. *Not even because of Cetterick – if it had been Britus who murdered him, or Rory, or Oisín, I wouldn't have cared; they all had good reasons to kill Cetterick. But all Bran wanted was to steal. He's low and deceitful and disgusting and I was right to hate him.* She thought of Bran's plans for her, the feel of his hot breath on her face, and she shuddered violently.

'Go on, Primrose,' she screamed. 'Faster, girl!'

The wet wind was in her face, but she welcomed the sting of the rain. She could see Bran up ahead, his purple cloak soaked almost black. He was beating his fat pony mercilessly with his whip, but Rory was gaining on him and Fergal wasn't far behind.

With one huge leap, Rory's horse was level with Bran. Bran had his knife out, but Rory raised his own whip and slashed him across the head. 'I'll hold your horse, Rory!' yelled Fergal. He leaned from his pony and seized Rory's horse by the bridle to keep it steady. Rory, his hands freed, dragged Bran off his pony, then jumped down, shoved Bran to the ground and tied his arms behind his back with a length of rope from his own saddlebag.

'Now,' he said grimly, 'let's take you back to the Brehon and see what you have to say for yourself.'

During the ride back to Drumshee, Ita stayed well behind the other three. She felt that she could never bear to look at Bran again, or to feel his eyes on her; she felt as if all she wanted to do was get into bed and pull the covers over her head and stay there for a month. It was only when Rory had handed Bran over to an astonished Owen, and Fergal had gone running to find Flann, that she managed to pull herself together and thank Rory for helping them.

'Don't mention it,' he said. 'It was a pleasure.' He looked as if he was about to ride off, but at the gate of the enclosure he turned his horse around. 'Ita,' he mumbled, 'I wonder if you'd do me a great favour. Would you tell the Brehon something for me?'

'Yes, of course,' said Ita mechanically, still thinking longingly of her bed.

'Could you tell your father . . .' said Rory hesitantly. 'Could you tell your father that I told him a lie the other day? I didn't go fishing. You see, the story I told about killing Naoise because of an argument over copper and gold . . . well, that wasn't the whole story. There was bad blood between Naoise and me. We were both in love with the same girl, and it all boiled over that night. I don't know if you know Niamh – she's the daughter of Cian, the fisherman who lives beside the little cove outside Liscannor Bay. Well, Cian wanted Niamh to marry Naoise – their families are old friends – so a betrothal was arranged; but she liked me better. Naoise and I got into a fight about it, and I – I killed him. I thought Niamh would never look at me again. But then we met at the fair at Coad, and I told her the whole story – and she forgave me. We have to meet secretly, because her father would kill her if he knew, so I swim around from Liscannor Bay into the little cove, and she waits for me there, in a cave on the beach. That's where I was on the day Cetterick was killed, but I didn't want to say so. That's why I made up that story. Will you tell your father?'

'Are you sure you don't want to tell him yourself?' she said, looking around to see if Fergal had managed to find Flann.

'No, no,' said Rory hurriedly. 'You'll do it better. You're clever – everyone knows that. Everyone says you'll make a great Brehon one day and we'll all be proud of you.'

Ita smiled. 'I'll tell him, then,' she said.

After Rory had galloped away, Ita stood for a moment looking through the great iron gates that led into the enclosure. This was where she had spent her life and where she had learnt to respect the law. Rory's words – *Everyone says you'll make a great Brehon one day and we'll all be proud of you* – rang in her ears. She straightened her back, held her head high, and walked in the gate without a glance at the cringing Bran. *The law must be upheld at all times, in all circumstances and in all places*, she said to herself as she went to find her father.

# Chapter 12

'But I didn't kill Cetterick,' insisted Bran. This was the sixth time he had said it. Ita looked around the schoolroom and saw nothing but scorn in the eyes of her fellow scholars. Everyone knew, or guessed, what had happened between him and Ita, and they were all impatient for Bran to be convicted and punished.

'But you stole the communion plate and cup.' Flann's voice was, as ever, carefully neutral. The cold anger that had shown in his eyes that morning, when Ita sobbed out the story of Bran's threats, was gone, replaced by his professional face. She had begged him not to tell Fionnuala, but Fionnuala had guessed; Ita had known that as, tight-lipped, the old woman fussed around her, pouring a hot bath, washing her hair and finally tucking her up in bed with a hot drink. And then her father had come in and sat by her bedside until she dropped off to sleep.

She wondered what had happened to Bran while she slept. Owen had been asked to guard him – perhaps the other boys had helped. Had he been interrogated? He had a purple bruise beginning to show around one eye. Had Owen done that? Or had it been Fergal, or Cathal, or Aidan? It hadn't been her father, Ita knew. He would have kept his anger under control. She would have to do the same. This was a matter of law now; she would have to banish all thoughts of what Bran had done, had threatened to do to her. *The law is there to discover the truth*, she repeated in her mind.

Aloud, she said, 'When you stole them, was Cetterick's body on the altar or on the floor?'

Bran turned to her with a look of hope struggling to the surface of his bruised face. To her annoyance, he began to sob.

'Ita, help me! I'm sorry. I would never have done anything to you . . . I didn't kill Cetterick, Ita. I was just joking when I said that. I . . . I was just trying to impress you.'

'Was Cetterick's body on the altar or on the floor when you stole the communion cup and plate?' repeated Ita stonily. 'Make him answer the question,' she said impatiently to her father.

'Answer the question,' said Flann. Ita saw a flicker of pride in his eyes as he glanced at her, and that helped her to steady herself.

Bran gulped. 'On the altar,' he said, wiping his wet

face with a piece of linen from his pouch. Ita avoided his pleading eyes and turned to her father.

'Could we send for Rua?' she asked. She didn't want to say more; her father might prefer to keep it a secret, for now, that Rua had put the body on the altar.

Flann nodded. 'Take Bran back to the stable and lock him in, Owen,' he ordered. 'Stay on guard. Diarmuid, ride over and ask Rua if he could spare the time to see me. Bring the mare for him to ride on.'

Owen took hold of Bran, who was still snivelling into his piece of linen, and jerked him to his feet, none too gently. The other boys averted their eyes from him. No one said anything until Flann left the room. Then they all crowded around Ita.

'You all right, Ita?' asked Cathal.

'That was a brilliant idea of yours,' said Ninian enthusiastically. 'I see what you're thinking. If the plate and cup were gone when Rua moved the body, then Bran is probably guilty.'

'I bet he is,' said Aidan. 'He'll be sent back to his father in disgrace, and we'll never have to see him again. It'll be just like the old days without him. I can't wait.'

'Tell us about the other stuff you saw, Ita,' said

Fergal. 'Where did he steal it all from?'

'I think he's been going around all the burial mounds and stealing from them,' said Ita. To her surprise, she no longer felt so angry at Bran. Now that she had her father and her friends around her and he was no longer a threat, she almost felt sorry for him. 'He probably found one by accident, then went looking for the others. Then he stole a silver chessman from my father, and then he went to the church to steal the plate and cup that King Carthen gave to Cetterick.'

'And then,' broke in Cathal, his words tumbling out in his enthusiasm, 'Cetterick came into the church and found him stealing. He probably threatened him with the Christian law – I think they have a law that it's a special crime to steal from a church – so Bran killed Cetterick, and came back here looking as innocent as a newborn lamb.'

'What do you think, Fergal?' asked Ita.

Fergal looked thoughtful. 'I don't think we can be sure of anything until we see Rua,' he said. 'Everything depends on whether the plate and cup were still there when he put the body on the altar.'

'Let's have a game of hurling while we're waiting,' proposed Cathal.

'Good idea,' said Ita. She hadn't played hurling for

quite a while, but suddenly she wanted to. She didn't want to think about Bran, or about Mahon, and it was impossible to think while you were running around a field whacking at a small leather ball. 'Come on, Fergal,' she said eagerly, pulling up her tunic over her belt so that it was well above her ankles. 'You and me and Ninian against Aidan and Cathal.'

Everyone was hot and flushed by the time Diarmuid arrived back with Rua. Flann came out to greet the druid, helped him dismount from the mare and escorted him into the schoolhouse with hospitable offers of drink and food. The law students looked at each other uncertainly, unsure whether they were allowed to follow or whether Flann would want to interview Rua in private.

'Well, he's left the door open,' said Ita in a low voice. 'Let's go in. I want to know what he says.'

The others followed her into the schoolhouse, and they sat down quickly on their stools at the table. Flann said something to Diarmuid in a low voice; Diarmuid ran across the enclosure and returned with Owen and Bran. Bran's hands were tied behind his back with a piece of dirty rope – Ita shuddered, remembering how hers had been tied like that only a few hours earlier.

'Rua, you told me you went into the church on

the morning of Cetterick's death,' Flann began quietly. 'Did you know that Cetterick kept a gold plate and cup, given to him by the king, in a small cupboard behind the altar?'

'I knew that,' said Rua. A quick expression of annoyance crossed his face.

'Can you tell us if you remember whether the gold plate and cup were still in their cupboard when you went in?' asked Flann.

Rua considered this question for a long time. Ita held her breath. She wasn't sure what she wanted his answer to be. In many ways it would be simplest if Bran had murdered Cetterick – but, almost in spite of herself, Ita didn't believe that he had. He was a liar and a thief, but she didn't think he had the courage to murder anyone – to lift that heavy candlestick and smash it down on a man's head. She looked around the room. All the boys were leaning forward on their stools, their faces eager and interested. None of them cared about Bran. Everyone wanted the murder solved, Bran banished, and their lives back to the pleasant way they had been before he arrived.

'The cupboard was as always,' said Rua eventually. 'The little door was shut.'

'Thank you,' said Flann gravely.

He turned to Bran. 'Bran, I find you not guilty of

murder, but I find you guilty of theft. You stole from the dead, you stole from the church and you stole from me. I will not keep a thief at my law school. Owen, take two of the men from the fields, take with you food and whatever you need, and return Bran to his father in Cork – keep him bound until you do so. Tell his father all of what has happened. Tell him that he will need to make restitution to the king, in his son's name, for the theft of the communion plate and cup; for my part, I want no restitution.'

The room was very silent after Owen led out the sobbing Bran. All his superior airs had vanished; he seemed to have crumpled into a small boy. The others looked at one another uncomfortably. The verdict was right and just, but the question hung in the air: who had killed Cetterick?

Flann was looking thoughtfully at Rua. 'You spoke of "the wronged one",' he said abruptly. 'Who was the wronged one you saw as you came to the church?'

Rua's face assumed the lofty look that it wore when he was going to prophesy, and Ninian moved impatiently.

'We have to know the truth,' said Flann gravely. 'The innocent must not suffer for the guilty.'

'Cetterick wronged many people,' said Rua sternly.

'But which one did you see?' said Ita. She hadn't known she was going to say it aloud until the words left her lips. Rua looked as shocked as if one of the stone images in the sacred wood had spoken.

'Cetterick's daughter.' He said it very simply, almost as if the words had been startled out of him. 'I did not know, then, that she was his daughter,' he added. 'I heard that later.'

Almost to himself, he said, in a dreamy voice, 'And then I understood . . . I saw her wash the blood from her hands, the blood of her father – but was he a father to her? Tell me that, Brehon.'

Without waiting for an answer, he got up, bowed courteously to Flann and said quietly, 'I'll walk back. Your boy need not trouble to accompany me.'

There was a moment's silence after Rua left the room.

'She couldn't – a girl like that!' burst out Cathal.

'Look at the evidence, Cathal; don't let feelings rule you.' Flann's voice was dry. Only Ita, who knew him best, could see the shadow in his eyes.

'Mara was there at the right time,' said Fergal. 'And Oisín also saw her washing blood from her hands.'

'She had a motive,' said Diarmuid. 'She must have hated her father terribly for deserting them. And then he refused even to give her a piece of silver . . .'

'And she's strong enough to do it,' said Aidan reluctantly. 'I saw her helping Mahon with those heavy flagstones at his house. And we saw that Ita was able to bring the candlestick down on the gorse bush. Mara is taller and stronger than Ita.'

'She has the character, too,' observed Ninian in his cool, detached manner. 'I never thought Britus did. He might have killed Cetterick on the spur of the moment, without meaning to do it, but he would never have been able to stop himself owning up. Mara's tougher.'

'What about her uncle, Donal the physician?' asked Ita. 'Are we still suspecting him?'

Diarmuid shook his head. 'No,' he said. 'His story was true: he'd just come back from tending to a wounded child. The boy's father remembers that Donal got blood on his tunic.'

Ita's troubled eyes met her father's. 'It would be a terrible thing if Mara were guilty,' she said. 'Under Brehon law, she would be put out to sea in a boat with no oars; under Christian law she would be put to death.'

Flann looked at her gravely. 'You would not want that to happen?' he asked.

Suddenly Ita felt a rush of gladness. No, she realised: she didn't want it to happen. She shook her head.

'Mara and Mahon want to get married,' she said steadily. 'I want every happiness for them both.'

Fergal reached under the table and squeezed her hand. She let her hand stay in his. It felt warm, and comfortable, and safe there.

Flann nodded. 'I think we all want that.' He thought for a moment. 'Tomorrow I must go see the king. I'll put all the facts before him. It would be best, I think, if the case were judged by Christian law. Brehon law gives no clemency in the case of *fingal*; Christian law may be more merciful, especially to someone of Mara's age and sex. I don't know, but I'll do my best.'

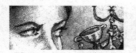# Chapter 13

With Owen gone to Cork and Flann preparing to go to the king's court, the scholars at Drumshee had a rare day off from their studies. It was a clear, bright day with a touch of autumn frost in the air, and Cathal, who had been out for an early-morning ride on his pony, came bursting in at breakfast time with the news that Malachy had organised a fox-hunt and they were all welcome to go.

'Great,' said Ninian. 'I'll come.'

'Me, too,' said Diarmuid, through a mouthful of porridge.

'And me,' said Aidan.

'Will you come, Ita?' asked Fergal anxiously. 'I know you don't like fox-hunting, but it would do you good.'

'The lad's right,' said Fionnuala. 'A day in the air will do you good. You're looking very pale.'

'We'll keep to the back, if you like,' said Fergal. 'Or, if you don't want to come, I'll stay at home with you.'

The other boys looked at him in astonishment. They were all fond of Ita, and they were feeling sorry for her at the moment, but to give up a day's hunting seemed unnecessarily heroic.

'You go with the others, Fergal,' said Ita hurriedly. 'I'll catch up with you. I just want to have a word with my father before he goes off to see the king.'

Sombrely she watched them all ride off, whooping and clowning, full of delight at their unexpected holiday. Cathal had managed to borrow a battered old horn from Fionnuala's husband Donogh, and they were hardly out of sight when Ita heard the horn being blown and the excited shrieks of the boys.

'They've seen a fox already,' exclaimed Fionnuala, coming out from the kitchen-house wiping her hands on her coarse linen apron.

'They won't be able to kill it,' said Ita with relief. 'They can't have met up with Malachy and the dogs yet.' Quickly she hitched up her tunic, tightening her belt to hold the loose folds out of her way, and ran to climb the old ash tree that grew outside the walls of the fort. The whole scene was spread out before her. Outside a clump of bushes on the hillside, three small foxes and one larger one were standing frozen with fear. The larger one – the mother fox, Ita thought –

had one paw raised, and her head was moving as she sniffed the wind. The boys were downwind of her, so she hadn't yet caught their smell, but she knew the sound of the horn. In the blink of an eye, the three smaller foxes – this year's cubs – had disappeared into the clump of bushes, and the mother fox ran off in the opposite direction.

She's not even trying to hide or go to ground, thought Ita. *She's leading the boys away from her cubs.*

'What's happening?' called Fionnuala from below.

'They've seen a fox,' Ita shouted back. 'They won't catch her, though. Malachy and the dogs are a long way off. I can't see them, but I can just hear them . . . Wait a minute – yes, I can see them. They're over by Drummoher.'

Fionnuala lost interest and went back to the kitchen-house, but Ita stayed in the tree, watching. She could hardly help cheering the fox on. The fox was up to every trick. She doubled back on her tracks, forcing the hunters to turn sharply; she ran uphill, making sure they could see her, then disappeared for a minute and reappeared a few hundred yards further down the hill. Again and again the horn sounded – and all the time the mother fox was leading the hunters further and further away from the cubs.

And she's so beautiful, thought Ita. In the late-summer sun the fox's coat shone red-gold. Its shining splendour reminded Ita of Mara's beautiful hair; she remembered how, when Mara had lurked outside Drumshee waiting to see what would happen to Britus, she and Aidan had thought Mara was a fox . . .

Suddenly Ita caught her breath in a gasp so loud that she looked down to see whether Fionnuala had heard it and come rushing out of the kitchen-house. Her heart started to thud, and her hands clutched the smooth grey bark of the ash tree. She looked back at the small figure of the red-gold mother fox, ducking and weaving, doubling back and leaping forward, always keeping within view of the shouting hunters and their dogs, and always leading them further and further away from the den where her cubs lay hidden.

'So that was it,' she said aloud. She stayed there for a few minutes, carefully going over everything in her head. Then she nodded once. Slowly she climbed down from the tree and walked across the enclosure towards the Brehon's house.

Flann was still inside, fastening his best cloak with the brooch of gold and silver that he always wore when visiting the king. Once again Ita was struck by the drawn look on his face. He was hating this. He couldn't bear the idea of causing the death of a girl not much older than his own daughter. And yet the pursuit of truth was carrying him along.

A great wave of happiness swept over Ita. It was like bringing a game of chess to a triumphant conclusion, like that wonderful moment before she spoke the word 'checkmate'.

'You can take off your cloak, Father,' she said. 'You won't need to see the king. Cetterick's murder wasn't *fingal*. Mara didn't kill her father. I know what happened. I've worked it all out.'

Without taking his eyes from her face, Flann unpinned the brooch, took off his cloak, folded it carefully and placed both cloak and brooch in the wooden chest beneath the window. Then he sat down on his chair by the fire. Ita sat down opposite him. She gave her father a reassuring smile; she felt calm and confident. He watched her with a puzzled air.

'So you didn't go fox-hunting with the lads, then,' he said after a minute's silence.

Ita seized the opportunity. 'I was watching them, though,' she said. 'It was the fox that made me understand. It was a mother fox, and its fur reminded me of Mara's hair – it's the same red-gold colour. It was keeping in the boys' sight all the time, deliberately attracting their attention; and all the time it was leading them away from its cubs. That's what Mara's been doing with us, Father.'

'You mean she was leading us away from the real murderer? But who would she protect? Her mother was nowhere near the church; I checked with a farmer who lives near them, and Grana was at home all day. Donal? I don't think so; we know where he was, too.'

Ita said nothing. Her father was feeling his way to the truth. She would give him a chance. She hoped he wouldn't guess – she wanted the triumph of telling him – though the truth seemed so obvious to her now that she couldn't understand why she hadn't thought of it earlier. Her hazel eyes sparkled as she looked at Flann. She held her breath; but he shook his head, a puzzled frown on his face.

'No,' he said. 'No, she must be guilty. Oisín and Rua are both sure it was blood she was washing from her hands. How can you explain that away?'

'Of course she was washing blood from her hands!' cried Ita. 'Don't you see what happened? She came to the church just after Cetterick was killed. She probably touched him, felt him – just to make sure he was really dead, I suppose.'

'But who killed him, then?'

'Britus, of course,' said Ita. 'Cetterick beat him once too often; he snapped, grabbed the candlestick and hit Cetterick over the head. When Mara came back in, she found her father dead and Britus probably almost dead from fear of what might happen to him. So she took charge.' Despite herself, she felt an immense admiration, almost affection, for Mara. She had managed it all very cleverly – and it had been both kind and noble of her to put herself in danger to save her father's slave boy.

'She told Britus what to do, of course,' she continued. 'She told him to go to Mahon and pretend that nothing had happened.'

'Why did she wait around, then?' asked Flann, still puzzled. 'Why didn't she go straight back to Lake Inchicronan and hope no one had seen her?'

'I think she felt responsible for Britus,' said Ita slowly. 'He probably told her everything – how Cetterick had treated him, how he had been driven to madness – so she felt that, as Cetterick's daughter, she was responsible for making sure he came to no harm. She's very brave and very clever, and I think she probably enjoyed getting the better of us all.

'She waited around to see what would happen when the body was found. When she saw Britus being brought here, and she knew he was in trouble, she just walked in and said she was the one who had found the body.'

'It could be,' said Flann, almost in a whisper. 'In any case,' he added, rising to his feet, 'I think I need to see both Britus and Mara.'

'Do you think I'm right?' asked Ita eagerly, as he took down his ordinary cloak from its peg on the wall.

Flann nodded. 'It makes sense. Somehow I always felt that this was a blow struck in anger – and I think Mara is too cool, too quick-thinking, to act like that. She would have turned her back on her father and walked out. But if Britus did it in a moment of desperation . . . that fits much better. What's going to happen to him now is another matter, but I think I can persuade the king to be merciful. Anyway, the first thing to do is talk to Britus and find out the truth.'

'I'll come with you,' said Ita.

'Are you sure?' asked Flann gravely. 'Mahon will probably be there, you know. Does it give you pain to see them together?'

Ita shook her head, then reluctantly nodded. 'I'm getting used to it, though,' she told him. 'I don't mind as much as I did a day or so ago. Too many things have happened since then.' Her mind went to that terrible time in the cave with Bran, when she had thought she was in his power; then it slid to the memory of Fergal carrying her away. A surprisingly warm feeling flickered inside her at the thought, and she smiled into her father's worried face.

'I'll get over it,' she said, in as matter-of-fact a tone as she could manage. 'I'm not the first girl in the world this has happened to. It's as well that we weren't married already. I wouldn't like to get divorced.'

Flann nodded, and put an arm around her shoulders as he led the way out of the house. He mounted his horse, and Ita tucked up her tunic and got onto Primrose.

Neither of them said much as they set out towards Inchicronan Lake. Flann was lost in thought, and Ita kept her mind fixed on the distant sounds of the hunt on the lakeland. She could hear the excited shouts, the frenzied barking of the dogs, and then, loud and clear, one long wailing note from the horn.

'She's got away,' she said with relief. 'The fox, I mean. She must have tricked them again. The dogs have lost her.'

They were on higher ground now, and they could look down on the plain before them. The fox had, indeed, got away. The horses and ponies were circling around, their riders talking and pointing in various directions; the dogs were lying down, panting, a few of them lapping from the lake.

'They'll find another fox,' said Flann with indifference. 'None of them will want to give up hunting on a fine day like this. They'll be off again in a minute.'

One of the hunters had given up, though. Fergal had looked up and seen Ita and Flann, and was riding towards them. Ita sat and waited, looking with pleasure at the small dark face she had known for most of her life.

'I'm tired of hunting,' Fergal said as he came near. He looked at Flann with a slightly puzzled air. 'Are you going to the king, Master?'

Flann shook his head. 'No,' he said. 'Ita has a new idea about the murder. I'm going to Inchicronan to question Britus and Mara again.'

'Oh,' said Fergal. He glanced at Ita, and she saw the concerned, protective look in his dark eyes. Once again, she felt a happy, warm glow deep inside.

'I was going to ask you if you'd ride to Liscannor with me,' he said. 'Would you like to come? It's a great day for the sea.'

'Yes, go,' said Flann. 'I'll probably be better on my own. I'll tell you all about it when I come back.'

Suddenly Ita found herself smiling. It would be difficult seeing Mahon with Mara. She was glad not to go. She would enjoy a gallop to the sea with Fergal.

'Yes, go on,' urged Flann. 'You can tell Fergal all about your idea on the way.'

'Let's gallop,' shouted Ita, as they turned their ponies back in the direction of the sea. She didn't really want to talk about Mara. She kicked Primrose gently with her heels and shot off, leaving Fergal to follow. He caught up with her in a minute, and they rode shoulder to shoulder along the roadway. Neither of them said anything until they turned onto the Ballagh road.

The Ballagh road was a broad ledge along the side of the hill, and it gave them a view of the whole plain stretching across to the Cliffs of Moher and the little bay of Liscannor. It was a clear day, and the figures of the men labouring in the fields or driving their cows stood out sharply, lit by the brilliant late-summer sun. She and Fergal weren't the only people riding towards the sea, Ita noticed. About a mile away, three other people were riding in the same direction. Two of them were youths dressed in the usual white tunics, but the third – a girl – was unmistakable. The light wind blowing in from the west lifted the cloud of her hair – hair like spun gold, with threads of red deepening and intensifying its brilliance. It was Mara, and with her were Mahon and Britus.

'Look,' Fergal said, pointing. 'Your father will have a wasted journey; Mara and Britus are there. It looks like they're riding towards the sea as well.'

Ita drew in a deep breath. 'Slow down, Fergal. Let them get ahead.' Almost to herself, she added, 'It looks as if the fox is playing one last trick.'

Then, when he turned to her in puzzlement, she told him the whole story: how she had guessed that Britus had committed the murder; how Mara, like the mother fox leading the hunt away from her cubs, had led suspicion away from Britus and towards herself. 'And now,' she finished, 'you can guess what she's going to do.'

'What?' asked Fergal.

'Look,' said Ita. She lifted her hand from the pony's back and pointed.

The sea was a dark blue, with small white waves ruffling its surface. And coming into the bay of Liscannor was a sea-going boat with white sails.

'She's going to get Britus away,' she said. 'She's going to send him back to his own people.'

'What shall we do?' asked Fergal.

'Just say goodbye,' said Ita with a smile.

By the time their ponies came down the path to the little rocky harbour, the boat had already started on its way back out to sea. Mara and Mahon were standing hand in hand, gazing out to sea and waving at the small figure in the stern of the boat. At the sound of the ponies' hoofbeats, they turned. Ita and Fergal tied their ponies to the iron ring in the harbour wall and walked down to meet Mara and Mahon.

'I've sent Britus back to his own people,' said Mara defiantly.

'I know,' said Ita. 'And I know how you shielded him. My father knows the truth, too; he'll tell the king. You were very brave and very clever,' she added, and to her surprise she found that the words came easily.

Mara studied her face and then smiled, an open, frank smile. 'Friends?' she said.

'Friends,' replied Ita. She took Fergal's hand and laughed a little, with a secret inner satisfaction, at Mahon's surprised face.

'Let's all ride back together,' she said. 'We have a lot to talk about.'

Look out for the next book
in Cora Harrison's Drumshee Chronicles

TREACHERY AT MIDNIGHT

And I took his body in my arms, and I carried him up to
the top of Mount Callan. And I laid him in the shallow
grave that I had hollowed out of the stony soil. And then
I shovelled the earth over him and hid him forever.
I carried over a heavy flagstone and placed it on the
mound. And with my knife I carved these words:

> *Here lies Conan, the fierce and turbulent.*

Who was Conan?

In the eighth-century turmoil of warring tribes, love,
jealousy, blackmail and revenge, Conan's story unfolds.
He entangles his foster brother, Columba, and the
beautiful Sorcha in a terrifying adventure that will
change all their lives forever.